www.tredition.de

AF196923

EVE SCHAUBERG

LORELEY

Rock Siren

www.tredition.de

© 2020 Eve Schauberg

Verlag und Druck: tredition GmbH, Halenreie 40-44, 22359 Hamburg

ISBN
Paperback: 978-3-7497-3436-8
Hardcover: 978-3-7497-3437-5
e-Book: 978-3-7497-3438-2

Loreley - Rock Siren

Eve Schauberg

Eve Schauberg, a writer from Germany. Working as creative director, she switched more to writing; diving deep in the underwater worlds to proof some of storytelling philosophies. Fascinated for the german Loreley mythos, she worked on this thriller for 7 Years. In hope to inspire young creatives around the globe to fight for their dreams with her rocky paranormal romance series.

"LORELEY – ROCK SIREN"

For my star 19-09-19

For my blue sky 12-05-81

Fo my life 11-07-52

Lia – I'm you, you are me

I thank Jasmin Lee my great horror co-writer, I loved to work with Jaze, she helped me to expand

on the original Loreley legend.

Tanks for my loved ghosts Lois Botwe,

Tiko Tolordava, Ranyas Senestela

And greatest editor in universe Candi Segress

loreleybook.com

Loreley Saga

Chapter 1

I fall down deep into the dark water.

I descent twice: first as a rocky young girl trying to save my dead love; and then again as a cursed siren to hunt.

Last night, I dreamt that I chopped Jim up into a hundred little pieces and ate them, one by one. Is it just my mad visions? But the Loreley curse really exists, I know it. Why the evil ghost chose me?

I will write about it in my song, as a rock musician, I have to.

Rock siren

Rain pelted the deck of a lone vessel, the hull of the ship crashing against the treacherous waves it was riding upon. The year was 1387, the wooden forged ship moaning in distress at the course of rough waves abusing it's every side.

The thunder boomed loudly overhead, the pitch-black illuminated only by the brief cracks of lightning.

What seemed louder than the deafening thunder, louder than the sounds of the waves crashing into the side of the ship. Louder than all of the chaos that surrounded were the broken-hearted sobs of a young girl.

She was just 17, the cries tumbling out of her lips were the sort that no child of her age should know. Knees bent and elevated off of the slippery wooden planks of the deck, the only thing keeping her suspended were the two large, burly men at her sides, grasping her upper arms firmly in their fists.

The bruising sensation of their fingers wrapped around her biceps would have been cause for concern, but the young girl, Loreley, had bigger issues at this point in time. With the howling winds and the pelting rain, her dress clung to her body like a second skin. With the soaked fabric clinging to her skin, her belly, swollen with child, was on display.

The reason for her cries? You might ask?

The man that paced along the tilting deck before her fatigued body. Dressed in regal clothing fitting of a man of his stature, an Earl, he sighed quietly, adjusting the hat atop his head which didn't do much to shield his face from the downpour of rain.

"Is it him?"

The Earl spoke up, hands folded calmly behind his back as he slowly paced back and forth over the deck. His brows furrowing in irritation when Loreley refused to reply. The Earl, Angler, had a short span of patience and an even shorter temper.

The heels of his expensive, leather boots clacking against the slick wooden panels of the desk as he marched towards her. Fingers decorated with rings balled into fists at his sides, swinging back and forth slowly with every intimidating step that the male took. The muscles in his jaw twitched as he ground his teeth together, glaring down at the vulnerable young woman in front of him with a fierce look in his eye.

The droplets cascading off of the rim of the hat poured onto her already soaked face, adding more insult to injury.

His hands, that of a man who never had to work a day in his life, reached out, burying themselves in her drenched, messy locks of hair.

Loreley tried to choke down her grunt of pain as Angler pulled her head up roughly, she didn't want to give this man the satisfaction of knowing that he had hurt her.

"Let me ask you again", he growled through his clenched jaws.

With his tight grip on the pregnant teen's hair, he gave a rough jerk of his hand, lifting her head forcefully so she would finally raise her gaze to the area in front of her.

More than her own suffering, more than her own turmoil, the sight before her was gut-wrenching. Hands tight behind his back, shirt ripped open and freezing drenched skin riddled with bruises. Tied from the top of the mast, was a noose around his neck.

His knees trembled with the effort it took to keep himself upright, should his fatigued legs give out, the noose would tighten around his throat and he would surely perish.

From the look of his torn clothes, it was clear to see he was of noble descent, his face rubbed raw from the rough fraying rope tied securely around his face, mouth forced to bite down upon it. His hair was a mess, matted to his forehead with the force of the rain. His eyelids were heavy, exhausted from what the brutes had put him through.

"Let me repeat myself, yes?"

Angler spoke up, dragging her attention away from the man tied up before her.

"Is he the father of your child or not?!" The Earl interrogated with exasperation in his voice.

The noble man, hanging onto his last legs of life panted shakily through his nose when Loreley met his gaze, she saw the way he mustered the last of his energy to slowly shake his head from side to side.

Despite how hard it had become to see with the rain pouring down and pelting against the floorboards, despite the fact that her hair slapping at her eyes was painful and nearly blinding, she could see this action clear as day. His message was clear, she had to keep quiet, for her own sake.

Hiccuping shakily, she glanced back down to the floorboards beneath her, she wouldn't answer.

Angler only grew angrier, even threatening the life of the potential father to her baby wasn't enough to get an honest answer out of her.

"You're more trouble than you're worth" the Earl growled through clenched jaws.

Amidst his anger, eyes wide with his deranged rage, he reached down and grasped fistfuls of the thin nightgown covering her shivering body. With a grunt, he pulled at the fabric, it didn't take much for the fabric to tear open with a loud rip.

Loreley cried out, what little protection from the outdoors she had was now laying in tethers around her shoulders. She suppressed a gag as he laid a disgusting hand upon her swollen stomach, palms brushing over the goosebump coated skin.

"I would guess you're 6 months along" he mumbled, his eyes following the path that his hand trailed over her skin.

She shuddered in horror as he admired the way his hand brushed over her skin.

"This child of yours, it has Royal blood, I'm sure of it. I'll kill it, I swear I will" he growled, tearing his hand away from her stomach in disgust.

Angler's chest heaved with his anger, droplets of rain falling from his cupid's bow, melting into the raindrops on the floor of the deck. He leered his head off to the side, glaring at the opening of the cabin.

"Bring her in!" Angler roared.

With their superior's command, two burly men stepped out the doors, in their hands the arms of an elderly woman. They clutched her much the same way as they did Loreley, holding her up by her biceps, knees lifted off the ground.

The young woman gasped sharply, no longer taking notice that her bare body was exposed to the elements, the object of her fear and transgression directed to the old woman.

Though weak from the cold and the rough handling, the older woman slowly lifted her head. The force of the rain had her drenched within seconds, wrinkled eyes narrowing to see through the storm and lock eyes wih=th her daughter.

"My child--" she croaked, voice cracking with not only age but heartbreak.

"My darling pearl-- please, please tell me it's not true"

Loreley choked back a stop as she listened to her mother's desperate pleads, biting her lip and squeezing her eyes closed as she turned her head away. The young girl could no longer bear staring at her mother, knowing that the woman who had cared for her was broken-hearted over the life choices that Loreley had made.

Angler grit his teeth, brows furrowed and eyes narrowed at the sight of the young girl turning her head away. His irrational anger bubbled up in his pumping veins, baring his teeth to the wind he glared down at her.

Ring coated fingers reaching down to once again bury themselves in her matted hair, wrenching her head up, ignoring the pained cry that escaped her lips.

"Why do you refuse to do as I say, you ignorant wench!"

It was as though the male had lost his grip on reality, drowning in his own rage. Jaw clenched in anger, whitened teeth bore to the wind, he lifted his leg, and with no concern for human life, he wrenched a powerful kick to the pregnant girl's swollen stomach.

Loreley's eyes widened, she could feel the way her expanded stomach caved as the Earl's metal-tipped shoe dug into her skin. The wind was knocked out of her lungs, the force of the kick pushing bile up her throat, vomit pouring from her trembling lips, splattering against the deck beneath her.

Gasping a desperate breath into her beaten lungs, Loreley cried out in pain, her stomach pulsing with pain and the possible loss of her unborn child.

"P-please no--" she gasped out, thickened saliva dripping off her blue lips as she remained bowed over, cradling her injured stomach against her knees.

"I-It's him" she choked out shakily, her voice choking up in her throat.

"I love him!" Loreley cried out, lifting her head and glaring the man before her in the eyes, "let him go".

Angler, satisfied that the young woman had finally given in and replied to him honestly. Sighing in content, his tense shoulders relaxing with a slump. The male hummed in content and reached down to brush the back of his knuckles against her freezing cheek.

"Good girl" he purred.

The young girl's stomach turned in disgust to feel his fingers against her vulnerable skin, she glared up at him, spitting a mouth full of saliva at the polished top of his shoes.

His pleased smile shifted to a wicked snarl and he huffed.

"You want us to let him go? Very well then."

Angler rose his hand, at the signal, the boy was turned around the mast, dangling feet placed atop a plank overlooking the swirling waters. The noose around his neck slipped down around his body, tying firmly around his ankles.

The men who had moved his body paused once they had finished their tasks, turning to their master to wait for their next command.

Angler, still with his hand in the air, glanced down at the young girl, his smile twisted in horrid amusement at the horrified expression on her face to see the scene playing out in front of her. He kept her waiting, waiting until a sense of hope bubbled up in her beaten chest.

He waited until he saw some sort of fire blazing in her eyes with the hope and knowledge that perhaps this man wouldn't go so far.

That was when he gave the signal.

Clenching his outstretched fingers in a sudden fist, the men handling Loreley's lover tensed and jumped into action. The larger of the two men kicked at the railing, watching with a grin as wicked as his master's, as the board holding the noble man's body up tumbled into the hungry waters below.

The man on the plank wavered as the plank beneath his feet slipped out from underneath him. Heart dropping into her stomach, Loreley could only watch as the board collapsed, crushed into a thousand pieces by the brutal waves and the father of her child toppled over the edge.

His body jerked to stop mid-fall, saved by the noose wrapped firmly around his ankles. With the force of the fall and the swing of the rope, his body collided with the body of the ship. A pained cry echoing over the thunder as he collided with the solid wood.

Loreley's arms jerked in the grip of the burly men towering over her, she cried out in horror as her beloved fell towards the river, the only sign of life was the tugging of the rope as he hung from the sail post.

All Angler offered was his snobbish chortle as he took in the misery he was causing, grin widening as he hears the sound of metal clinking against metal. The men were tying heavy metal chains around her lover's ankles, large metal ball balancing on the edge of the railing attached to the chains.

There was no denying that the Earl was taking pleasure in this, feeding off of the heartbreak and pain he forced onto those around him.

A sinister grin coiling at his cheeks, knowing the power that he wielded, it took a simple snap of his fingers for the men to react to his every wish.

Loreley didn't know what was more heartbreaking, the echoing sound of the click as the pad of his finger slapped against his palm; the sound of the blades as they sliced through the ropes; the sound of the chains as the weight of the man's falling body toppled the heavy metal ball over the edge; or the sound of the splash that came moments after.

All Loreley could hear was an awful deafening ringing in her young ears, she hadn't even acknowledged the scream that tore out her throat, had it not been for the sandpaper feeling of pain that coated the inside of her delicate throat.

Her eyes wide with horror, despite the rainfall that splashed against her waterline painfully, she didn't register any of the pain, she couldn't care less under the crushing weight of grief against her weakened heart.

Angler didn't spare her a moment to grieve, he couldn't care less about the pain that she was enduring, nor about the screams ripping from her empty lungs.

He rolled his eyes, pinning her antics down to overdramatic theatrics. With a nod of his head, the men gripping onto her arms dragged her back. Showing no signs of care to the fact they might potentially injure the young woman or her unborn child.

Loreley, too weak to stand on her own feet, too lost in the grief of the love of her life, simply fell onto her behind. Sobbing helplessly as she was dragged against the slippery floorboards back into the belly of the ship.

Although her heart was broken and her spirit was crushed, she seemed to be coming back to her senses as she was dragged into the ship. Not knowing the fate she might befall, the young woman cried out, she knew whatever fate they held for her was not a good one.

She kicked, thrashed and tried to wrench herself out of their grip, but they were strong, and with the freezing cold, the beatings and the heartbreak she was weak, too weak to release herself from their grip no matter how hard she tried.

Their grip bruising on her upper arms, they were ruthless, dragging her down the steps, ignoring her cries as her tail bone banged painfully against the edge of each step during their long descent. Her eyes screwed up in agony as her bruised body was forced down the jagged edges of the staircase. Over the sound of her heart pounding in her chest, she could hear the distant whispers of voices she had never heard before.

She was being dragged down towards the basement of the ship, well underneath the waves crashing outside. The closer she got, the louder the whispers became. Swallowing down her cries of pain to focus on the whispers, she tried her best to distinguish the words, to focus on what was being said, to possibly decipher what her fate might be.

Thrown onto the floor, the bruising grip on her biceps finally relinquished, roughly tossed onto the hardwood floors below. With a pained whimper, the young woman slowly lifted herself on her shaky arms, reaching up to rub the forming bruises on her upper arms.

Between the groups of people, a hole was made for her, the figures, dressed in deep burgundy cloaks stepping away from her, simply watching as she scrambled to pull her torn dress together to hide her body from their view.

As Loreley got to glance around the room, the set up around her was one that sent alarm bells ringing in her head. There was a table in the center of the room, a large trough, running along the four corners of the table rested on the floor, supposedly there to collect anything that spilled from the table.

Black wax candles illuminated the small room, poised all around the long oak table. Fear settled in her heart, she prayed desperately that this wasn't what she thought it was. That the storybook picture of occult happenings wasn't painted out right before her eyes.

Fear froze at her heart in horror at what might become of her in this strange room filled with these strange people.

Their heads, hidden by their hoods, raised to look at the Earl slowly descending the stairs. He exuded an air of authority, their heads dipping towards the male. A hooded figure by the door bending over, hands extended with a folded black robe resting on his palms.

Angler reached out, grabbing the robe off of his palms without so much as a second glance to the man that had handed it to him. His superiority complex passing to even his peers.

The male stared down at the young woman on the floor, he was smug as he tied the black cloak around his neck. He knew that Loreley was growing more and more helpless, the hope of survival slowly draining from her eyes.

"Lift her"

With the simple command rolling off of Angler's tongue, the closest strangers reached down, gripping onto Loreley's delicate skin painfully tightly. They heaved her off of the ground, laying her down on the table in the center of the room.

They kept their grips on her wrist, preventing her from wrenching herself off of the table or daring to try and escape. Two more bodies rushed over, pinning down her thrashing ankles, blocking off any chance of escape that she had left.

Loreley wouldn't stop, even though she knew it was hopeless, kicking against their palms, trying to pull against their superior strength.

Over the sound of her own cries, she could hear the sounds of the familiar clicking of expensive shoes on the hardwood ground. Her body stilled, tensing immediately as the familiar face came into view.

Angler stared down at her, head tilting in amusement as he stared down at the young woman, admiring the distress on her face. Reaching down he runs his admiring fingers down her bruised stomach with a sigh of content.

"Finally we have what we need" he breathed out as he looked down at the exposed skin of her pregnant belly. His fingers praised the growing bruise on her stomach that he had caused.

"You're going to help us achieve our dream, so be a good little girl, sit there, and stay silent" he warned, eyes narrowed as he stared down at her.

Not knowing what was in store for her, she could only stare up at the male in debilitating fear. Sinking back into the table, pressing back against it to try and sink as far away from the Earl as she possibly could.

Angler stepped back, lifting his head as he looked over at his loyal subjects, nodding towards them.

"Bring the knife" he commanded.

Loreley's eyes only widened in horror at the command, head turned to watch as more of the hooded figures approached. In hand they held a large dagger, pulling off the leather sheath and tossing it aside carelessly.

Her restless struggling only increased, watching as they approached with blade in hand. She choked out desperate pleads, tears of horrified fear pouring down her cheeks. The number of people having to hold her down had doubled. Gripping onto her limbs by wrapping their arms around them, lessening the flailing with the force of their whole body.

Loreley thrashed to the best of her ability, throwing her head back and trying to twist her way out of their grip, but they were too strong and too plentiful. All she could do was lay there and wait for the pain to come.

And come it did.

A warm hand was braced against her overgrown stomach, the blade in hand, the cold metal touched her lower abdomen above her left hip. A gasp of panic choking the young woman as she tried desperately to pull from their grip, her eyes squeezed shut with a desperate sob.

Her eyes were as wide as moons when the blade began pressing into her skin, she wasn't quite sure if she felt the pain at that moment, or whether her brain and blocked it out for the possibility of maybe surviving through it all.

Despite the short-circuiting of her brain cutting off all sensations in the lower half of her body, she could still feel the way the blade slid over her skin, the warm blanket of blood pouring down from the incision made.

The blade was dropped onto the table with a clatter, splashing even more blood onto her already soaked body. The incision ran across the underside of her overgrown stomach, from hip to hip. Dagger discarded off to the side, they reached towards the large incision.

It was a feeling that Loreley was unable to describe, the sensation of hands slowly pushing through the incision and invading her body. The feeling of fingers holding her skin open so the arms could invade her insides. They showed no care for her body, no one noticed the way her eyes rolled into the back of her head in her agony, nor did they care.

When the fingers happened upon her organs, they were brutishly pushed out of the way, the punches of pained air leaving her lips went unnoticed.

They searched around, using her body as their personal anatomy plaything, before reaching into her womb, and finding what they had been searching for.

Although she had prayed that it wasn't the case, Loreley wasn't ignorant enough not to know what they were looking for. She was well aware that they had planned to steal her baby, to use her unborn child, the last piece of her lover, to perform some cruel, twisted occult acts.

Sinful hands wrapped around her child's pure body and carefully, her child was wrenched from her body.

She was only five months along, her head weak as she lifted it to get a glimpse of her child before it was lost to her forever. Premature, it was tiny, able to fit in the palm of one of the men with ease. Her child didn't cry, it didn't move, head and arms limp and dangling from the man's hand.

Surely the blow to her stomach did damage to her poor baby, with its lungs still under formed, and it's airways blocked by her amniotic fluids.

She reached out towards her child, or rather, she tried.

Her arms weak from the ordeal she was being forced through, too fatigued to fight against their shackles on her arms. All she could manage was the twitch of her fingers, drooping eyes following the path of her child as they carried it over towards the head of the table where there sat a large metal bowl.

Angler made his way over to it as the child was gently set inside, humming as he looked down at it, he reached out his hand silently.

One of his subjects hurried to grab the dagger off the table, wiping the blade off on his robe and gently lowering it in the male's palm with a bow of his hooded head.

Wrapping his ruthless fingers around the metal handle of the dagger, he stared down at the tiny, limp infant in the bowl before him.

"N-no--"

Was all that she had the energy to say, her head tipped back to try and see what they were doing to her baby. Although she knew it wasn't something she was going to want to see, some part of her thought that perhaps, if she was looking, that they might spare her child.

Her hope was fruitless, vision blurred by her fatigue and the seemingly never-ending tears building up in her waterline.

She could only watch in her weakened horror as Angler rose his arms above his heads, fingers wrapped around the handle of his blade. Eyes void of any emotion as he stared down at the bowl below him, he gave a twisted lick of the lips before plunging the blade into the bowl with a splatter.

It was silent in that moment, or rather, Loreley thought it was.

There was a loud, high pitched ringing in her ears.

Vaguely, she could register the feeling of her lungs running out of air. The raw insides of her throat stinging with pain as she watched Angler's monotonous response to the blood of a child now splattered against his cheek.

"Pray"

Were Angler's only words.

The cloaked figures around the body of the dying woman joined hands, their hands lowered towards the floor. Quietly, they began to mumble, in a language that Loreley didn't recognize. Powerless against them, all she could manage to do was watch, watch as Angler plunged the blade back into the bowl.

Over and over.

Over the sound of the ringing, the sound of the chanting, the sound of the ringing in her ears. She could hear the sounds of stomach-churning squelching each time the blade plunged into the bowl. The sound of trickling as blood slowly filled the metal chalice.

The young girl slumped against the table she had been laid out on, her eyes slipping closed as she pressed back against the blood-soaked wood.

The chanting only grew louder, the time between repetitions shortening, and as Angler threw the blade aside, they rose their connected hands above their heads in praise. They bowed and succumbed to the male's every whim, devoted to Angler wholeheartedly.

A sick grin on his face, blood soaking his hands, splattered on his cheeks and reflected in his eyes.

"Now, my people, we bring the blood of a royal child! Our offering to our Lord Amdusias!" he cried out.

Angler grasped the bowl tightly in his hands, reaching down to press his lips to the cold outer edge of the bowl in hand. Closing his eyes, head leaning back, he tipped the bowl towards his mouth, the warm fluids of her child flowed into his mouth.

He swallowed them down with a loud gulp, handing the bowl over to the person to his right for them to repeat his actions.

With blood trailing down the corner of his lips, he stared down at the mother of the child he had just murdered. With a twisted grin, teeth still coated in the remnant's of blood, he licked his lips slowly. He was making a mockery of it, of the death of her child that he had caused, at the death of herself that he was causing.

The chalice was passed to each robed figure standing around her, each took a gulp of blood of their own.

Angler was the first to have any sort of reaction, staring down at his hands as they trembled before him. Stumbling back as though he were intoxicated, his eyes wide with his manic insanity, a grin spreading across his blood-stained lips.

"Y-yes!" he cried out ecstatically.

"I-I can feel it" he breathed out as he stared down at his fingers, his eyes wide, lost in his own madness.

"The power I can feel it!" Angler reared his head back with a loud bout of laughter.

Jaw clenched together, he stared down at the young mother, grinning in his sadistic glee.

"We have no use for her anymore, toss her into the river, we've got what we needed. She can follow her lover into the afterlife." Angler commanded, waving his hand nonchalantly to get the dying teenager out of his sight.

The will to fight drained from her fatigued body, she was limp as the Earl's subjects lifted her up into their arms.

Besides the sound of their shoes against the hardwood floors as they carried her up the stairs, she could hear the sounds of her blood dripping, pouring onto the floor below out of her gaping incision. In that moment, she was both in the most amount of pain ever experienced, and equally, the least.

Loreley had lost everything dear to her that day. Her lover, her mother, and her unborn child. All had been ripped away in the hands of the Earl, Angler.

For a moment, she relished in the feeling of the cold rain thundering against her fragile skin. And though it was a brief taste of solace to be out of the room containing the man she despised, she felt nothing.

Numbed by the loss she had endured.

She felt no fear, even as she was lifted over the edge of the railing, a sheer drop leading towards the feisty waves below.

Even as their hands slipped out from under her, even as she began to plummet towards the water, she felt nothing.

Nothing but her boiling rage.

Before Loreley knew it, the crashing waved enveloped her broken body and in the blink of an eye, she had been swallowed into the deep. As she fell, the distant cry of her mother, screaming out her name echoed in her ears.

"Loreley!"

Although the pain of her lungs crushing under the weight of the waves as her oxygen levels continued to dwindle, she felt nothing but the sweet relief of death embrace her.

That was what Loreley had been expecting, death, but it wasn't what seemed to enfold her. What blanketed the young girl in its arms, was rebirth.

The water around her was eerily still despite the crashing above the surface, channels of water seeming to encase the young woman's body. Bubbles and currents tinted red with her blood. Head tipped back and arms spread wide, there was nothing worse than what she had already endured, so she willingly embraced the fate that was about to befall her.

From the deck of the ship, should you peer down into the water, one might catch a glimpse of the swirling storm beneath the surface. And should one look close enough, deep enough, should they lean over the railing protecting them from the icy waters, they might see a pair of glowing eyes staring right back at them.

Angler and his people had migrated back towards the deck, it had been a while since their offering was handed over to the demon of the thunder. Despite Angler's words that he had felt the power thrumming through him, their Lord still had yet to present himself.

The longer they stood around, the shorter Angler's patience became.

His head bowed constantly, hands clasped together and lips muttering in quiet prayer. Despite the rain that pelted their backs, they would not return indoors without explicit orders from the Earl. It was dangerous to be outside during such a fearsome storm, but Angler showed no concern, the safety of his subjects was the least of his worries.

"We gave you blood, we gave you the sacrifice, I beg of you my Lord, visit us, bless us with your power" he whispered beneath his breath.

Around him, devoted to their Earl, the other members began to chant and pray, beginning alongside their master for the Lord of the thunder to visit.

"Grant us with your power, show your presence, I beg of y-!"

Angler's ramblings were cut short, interrupted by the very thing he wished to control.

A shadow cast over the cult members scattered across the deck, raised high over their heads was a wall of water. A wave larger than any they had encountered before was fast approaching, too fast for them to have any hope of turning the ship and evading its path.

All heads rose to stare up at their impending doom, the water arching over the large ship as if it was only a fleck in the waves. Before they even had a chance to scream, the wave was crashing down against their ship.

The crew were swiped off their feet, swept into the hard flowing currents of the wave as it devoured the ship and everyone aboard.

Angler could only float in disbelief as he was dragged into the dark, cold depths of the river he had forced under his will.

The light streaming through the surface seemed to grow more and more distant, eventually, he couldn't quite tell which way was up any longer. Bubbles flowed from his lips, flowing up towards what he could only assume to be the surface.

Although his arms flailed and his legs kicked hopelessly, the weight of his robes dragged him down further.

From the faint rays of sunlight streaming through the wild surface of the water, he saw something flash across his vision. Struggling to position himself upright, cheeks puffed out with the air he had managed to drag into his lungs before submerging, he hurriedly turned in the water, trying his best to catch sight of what had swum in front of him.

Bubbles escaped his lips in his panic as he saw the silhouette flit past his vision once again. Whatever it was, it was growing closer, charging towards his fallen comrades and with a cloud of dark red fluid, tore the people around him limb from limb.

Angler was left to watch in shock and horror, as in the blink of an eye, the bodies of his devoted followers slowly began to float towards the surface, limp and lifeless. One by one they were ruthlessly slaughtered as they struggled to breach the surface of the water.

Before he knew it, they were all gone, in a split second, each life aboard the ship beside his own had been taken out. The silhouette in the distance paused, seeming to slowly turn towards the Earl, it was hard to make up, what with the edges of his vision shifting to black along with his lack of oxygen.

Gritting his teeth and squeezing his eyes closed he reached up towards his neck, eagerly tugging at the strings around his neck to try and relieve himself of the heavy weight dragging him towards the watery grave below him.

He willed himself not to suck in a breath of relief as the knot around his neck fell apart, the heavy cloak floating away from his body. He felt lighter in an instant, slowly drifting towards the surface, and as he peeked open his eyes to check where the beast had disappeared to, his eyes met the glowing orbs of the monster that had killed his crew.

His eyes widened, bubbles flying out of his mouth at the sudden appearance of the beast before him. He rushed back, trying to push himself as far away from the terrifying-looking creature as he could.

Slapping his hands over his mouth to prevent the extra air from escaping, Angler's eyes could only widen as he finally got a better look at the being before him.

He recognized that face, and it certainly recognized him too.

Glowing eyes narrowed in their hatred as they stared at the man before them.

It was Loreley, though not as Angler once knew her.

Her legs which had once been weak and bruised from the rough treatment she had endured were now fused, connected to one another, coated in iridescent scales and trailing off into a snake fin. She moved very fast.

She had transformed, what was once a vulnerable young teenage girl, was now a siren. Her blood as cold as her gaze as she glared at the cause of her sorrow.

Angler wanted to plead for his life, to grovel on his knees and beg for forgiveness. But how was he to do it? So many meters beneath the surface, with his lungs screaming for air and his eyes burning from the cold water.

With the look in her cold, glowing eyes, he knew that forgiveness wasn't an option. Not given so much as one more chance to shoot for the surface, her webbed fingers reached out towards him. Her fingernails narrowed into sharp points, perfect for cutting through the water, shot out towards him.

Too slow for her well-timed movements, he had no way of avoiding her movements, stiff in the water as her arm darted through the water.

His jaw fell slack, bubbles pouring out of his mouth as a muffled scream tore through the water. Her sharpened fingernails had shot out at his face, nails pressing into his eye sockets. His hands reached up to claw at her arms as he felt the way her cold fingers curled around his eyeball, slowly gouging them from their sockets.

What came next was worse.

Worse than the fact that he had been blinded in both eyes, his eyeballs gouged out by a set of sharp fingers, optic nerve severed with snapping jaws was the sound, and knowledge, of what she did with them.

Unable to see, hands pressing against his empty eye sockets, in some vain attempt to try and restore his vision. All he could do was listen, listen as his eyes were stuffed into the young girl's mouth, as her razor-sharp teeth chomped down on the ocular organs.

The outer film of his eyes split open with a pop, the sound of her jaws chewing down on them with a squelch made his stomach turn.

Fearing that he would suck in water should he begin dry heaving, the male used the opportunity to rush towards the surface.

Without the weight of his cloak dragging him down, he managed to find the surface with ease.

Head breaching the surface, he tipped his head back, coughing out the water that had entered his airways and gasping in an eager breath. His limbs waded in the water, keeping his head above the surface despite the ravaging waves.

Angler prayed that perhaps that was all she wanted, perhaps she needed nothing more besides his eyes, and hopefully, perhaps that was all the revenge she desired.

His hopeful prayers went unanswered, crushed by the simple pressure of a strong grip wrapping around his ankles, yanking him under the tide. His hands grappled at the surface of the water, attempting to claw at the surface of the water in hopes of survival.

However, his attempts were fruitless, in a swift tug, he was pulled beneath the waves. There was a moment of what could only be surmised as serenity, before, bubbling towards the surface of the water, was a cloud of crimson.

Angler didn't surface after that.

It was assumed all of the crew died that night, the destruction of the ship pinned down to the awful storm. However unbeknownst to the siren, in her rampage, tearing people limb from limb, slaughtering and torturing them, she had missed out on one.

Hands darted out of the ocean, trembling fingers gripping onto the smooth boulder, pulling himself from the cold depths and onto the lone boulder, was a fatigued older man, panting and heaving as he collapsed against the dry rock for a moment of peace.

-

3 Months had passed since the destruction of the ship.

3 months since the massacre that had occurred in the waters that fateful day.

Having witnessed her bleeding daughter being tossed into the river, Loreley's mother never gave up hope that her daughter might return that day.

Several fishermen told about mysterious encounters. They told of having seen the Loreley alive. Now, Loreley's mother sat, on a similar tug boat, with Loreley's father by her side, scouring through the waters in hopes of finding their daughter.

She turned to glance at the other male sitting in the boat, oars in hand, leading them out to the river. They had met him on the pier before setting sail and had asked to borrow his boat. When explaining the reason for wanting to go out, the male took on a grim expression.

The older woman was surprised to hear that he was no stranger, rather a survivor of the wreckage that had taken place that night. After hearing that the couple were Loreley's parents, he had offered to take them out into the sea, to the scene of the wreckage where he had seen Loreley last.

So they sat in the boat atop the water, the waves, significantly calmer than that day three months ago. The man had said nothing the whole journey, as soon as they had sat in his small sailboat, he took hold of the oars and began rowing.

Sweat was building on his forehead, head tipped down towards his knees, he grunted continuing to row under the beating sun. The look on his face was one she couldn't quite describe, one that must've been a look of trauma, even without looking he seemed to know where he was going. Surely the scene of the tragedy was burned into his mind.

"A tug boat?"

Loreley's mother heard her husband mumble curiously, she tore her gaze away from the stranger and gasped as she saw a lone boat, floating and bobbing along the waves slowly approaching their boat.

The man rowing lifted his head curiously, brows furrowing he hurriedly turned the angle of the oars to rush towards the boat. Perhaps there was another survivor?

As they approached the boat slowly, Loreley's mother gasped sharply, letting out a shaky cry of disbelief, leaning against her husband for support.

Even from the distance they stood, the horror of the inside of that small boat was clear. The light wood insides stained red, a small pool of nothing but crimson liquids filled the base of the boat. Laying within the pool, was a young girl, no older than 17, wearing nothing but the blood she was bathed in.

It was hard to see past the gruesomeness of it all, but as the boat grew closer, the could see under the blood coating her face.

"L- Loreley--" the older woman choked out.

They had thought that she was dead, lying so still in a pool of her own blood, but upon hearing the sound of her mother's voice, the young girl's eyes snapped open.

She sucked in a sharp breath and sat up hurriedly, rocking the boat with the force of the action. She stared wide-eyed at the people in the boat opposing her, not a hint of recognition in her eyes.

"Loreley -- my darling--"

As the older woman attempted the reach her hands out to the young woman, the teen bore her teeth with a loud hiss, turning around she threw herself into the water. Disappearing into the chilling depths leaving a cloud of red blood dispersing in the waves behind her.

"Loreley!"

"I would stop if I were you, Ma'am"

She jumped upon hearing the stranger speak up for the first time since leaving the shore. Gaze falling to the man he stared out at the waters their daughter had disappeared into.

"That ain't your daughter Ma'am, your daughter died that day three months ago" he mumbled gruffly, turning to meet her eyes with a piercing stare.

"That thing we just saw? That was a monster"

In the days that came, a story seemed to spread, the story of shipmates hearing a beautiful tune aboard their vessels, filing out onto the deck in time to witness a woman, a woman of superior beauty sitting upon the rocks. Her slender fingers combing through the long locks of gold hair atop her head.

They say she sang the sorrowful words of a love she had lost. Singing rhymes of her child and her love lost at the river. Along with the tale of the beautiful woman, came more tragedy, when the tide rose lives were lost. Sailors entranced by the beauty of her song drawn out into the water, disappearing for the rest of their days.

Sailors and tourists alike were given words of warning, for the beautiful beast that resides in the water has a hankering, she finds delight only in the flesh of man.

-

Many things had changed since that day 600 years ago, the year was now 2019, the port where the tragedy had taken place was recently turned into a popular tourists destination, strangers flocking to see if they could take sight of the beautiful woman that sat atop the rock and sang her song of death.

In her University appointed apartment, overlooking those very same docks, was a girl, ignorant to the legend that brought in such popularity with the tourists.

Her name was Lora. Hair the same, deep blue eyes, the same crisp brown, she was the spitting image of Loreley from all those years ago. Lora was completely unaware. She knew nothing of the tale, nothing of the tragedy that had taken place.

In her own blissful ignorance, the young woman lived out her days the way any exchange student might. Lora was lounging in the window of her living room, the warm sun filtering through the canopy of leaves outside. It was late September, the semester starting only a few short weeks ago and she had finally been able to get an apartment with her friend, Jenny. It was a small apartment, with a beautiful view of the campus, and quiet neighbors. Lora was in her third year of school here at the local pop art university and was finally able to live off-campus.

Her parents had passed away when she was a child and she had been raised by a reclusive aunt since then. It wasn't a normal childhood since her aunt lived in a small cliff-side cabin outside of the bigger city. She could still remember the smell of mint from her aunt's candy dish and the mewling of her three fat cats.

Unfortunately, her aunt had passed away during her first year of college and, when Lora went back to aunt's home to pack up her belongings and family heirlooms, she found that the cats had gone missing. Among her aunt's things were some important family documents that she felt should be kept as well.

The first was an old bible, dating back to the seventeenth century, with the names of all the family members starting with her mother's great-great-great-great grandparents. The Bible contained birthdays, death dates, and locations; Lora was quite surprised to find that her family had always been seafarers and fishermen in the Portland region. What also surprised her was the detailed recipes for random tinctures and potions stuffed into the back of the holy book. She could barely make out the scrawled, almost incomprehensible, language written on old pieces of parchment and paper.

The second item that she made sure to keep was a small photo album. It was from her mother's side of the family and had been passed down, from mother to daughter, almost as long as the bible had. The first photographs were from the late nineteenth century but before that were sketches, notes, and more random recipes for tinctures and apothecary potions. Lora had found this odd but took the books with her to her new apartment anyway, unwilling to part with distant relatives that were now all gone.

However, her student two-bedroom apartment with her best friend was wonderful. They had been used to living in dorms together, but it wasn't until now that Lora truly appreciated how tidy and well-organized her best friend was. Jenny, like Lora, took her schooling seriously and wanted to set herself up for a prosperous, and easy career. Jenny's father carried her bills and she also was popular with several talented and good-looking male students who had frequented their apartment recently. Jenny, unlike Lora, wasn't ready to settle down in a relationship and opted for casual dating instead.

Lora was still looking out the window, contemplating the changing leaves outside and the distant beaches beyond, when Jenny came home. She had her bag over her shoulder, she looked tired but greeted Lora with the same smile she always did.

"How were guitar classes this morning?" Jenny asked, setting her bag and coffee down on the countertop of the kitchen before sauntering over to the couch and flopping down on it.

"Good," Lora nodded, loving that all her classes were before noon throughout the week. "This semester will go well. I've got the best of the same professors from last year."

"I expect you'll ace everything," Jenny chuckled, folding her arms under her head like a pillow. She kicked off her shoes then, letting them fall to the floor from the end of the couch as she lounged there comfortably. "So, did you get your boyfriend aboard?"

"He'll be flying in two days from tomorrow," Lora smiled, feeling a blush spread over her face. Jenny noticed and giggled, turning on her side to prop herself up on her elbow.

"Do we need to talk about the danger of first fly?" Jenny teased, making Lora blush brighter.

"No," Lora affirmed, knowing exactly what Jenny was talking about. "I think I've got this."

"Anyway, it's not my type," Jenny smirked, glancing out the window. "I'm tired. Want to order some food, before we start tonight?"

"Sure," Lora nodded, standing from her chair near the window. "What do we want?"

"Whatever you are in the mood for," Jenny nodded, watching Lora cross the living room toward the corkboard where all the menus were hanging. "I'm hungry so I am up for anything."

"I think we should just order ourselves something simple," Lora mused, grabbing the menu for their favorite Thai place. "An order of vegetable Lo-Mein and some rice."

"Sounds amazing," Jenny sighed, lying back down and staring at the ceiling. "So, the boyfriend's name is Jack, right?"

"Yes, and he's an artist from Pennsylvania." Lora confirmed, picking up her cellphone to dial the order in. When she was done and had gotten the cash out for the delivery, she sat back down at the window, smiling sheepishly at Jenny. Jenny, on the other hand, looked positively roguish. She had a wide smirk and her eyebrows were raised in curiosity as she contemplated her friend.

"So, the first time ever meeting after a year, huh?" Jenny asked, watching her friend from her position lying on the big comfortable couch. "but you are still a virgin, and nervous?"

"Very," Lora admitted, tucking some hair behind her ear. "I mean, we've talked a lot and have video chatted so many times that it doesn't even feel like this is our first full meetup. It is scary and exciting all at the same time."

"I hate men, but he seems really nice," Jenny nodded. "And he's handsome too."

"You think so?" Lora asked, looking down at her phone. Her background picture was Jack, waving at her from a tourist monument in Pennsylvania.

"Are you kidding?" Jenny asked, looking positively bewildered. "Have you seen the man?"

"I have," Lora grinned, admiring the picture of her boyfriend now. He was tall, wired blond hair with green eyes and beautifully tanned skin. His jaw was square, his shoulders wide, and his muscles were intricately toned. He wasn't overly buff nor was he bulky; in fact, Lora thought he was quite average and that was her reason for being attracted to him in the first place. She had always found the beauty in things that to most people looked average. To her, he was a piece of art but apparently, Jenny even thought he was handsome.

"We're going to have to dress you up before you meet him, huhu," Jenny smirked, sitting up on the couch. "I've got a lovely underwear that I think would work beautifully with your figure. Show off all the right curves for them."

"I've got the perfect outfit picked out," Lora informed, crossing her arms over her chest. "I don't want to show off my curves anyway."

"You better show him your curves in a more private setting," her friend chuckled, reaching over and patting Lora's shoulder. "Don't worry about anything. He'll be so happy to see you that it won't even matter."

"I'm so excited," Lora admitted, looking up at her friend thankfully. "And nervous."

"What could you be nervous about?" Jenny asked, placing her hands on her hips. "You're gorgeous so it can't be that…"

"I don't know why I am so nervous, but I've been on edge ever since he told me he was coming to make it happen," she sighed, watching the sun setting outside their window. "I am so on edge these days…"

"Just relax," Jenny nodded, sitting on the arm of the couch to look at Lora. "You're just high-strung. It has been a rough couple of years for you since your aunt passed. You've been focused on your schooling and maintaining your relationship and it has completely worn you out. Just take a break or drop an extracurricular course if you want. You need some time for yourself or you're going to end up losing your mind."

"I know," Lora admitted, looking up at her friend. "It's just this foreboding that I can't shake. I haven't felt this way since I was a kid, you know?"

"You think the visions will return?" Jenny questioned, tapping her chin gently as she folded her arms across her torso. "Have you had any since your aunt's passing?"

"No," she sighed, looking back out the window. "Just the one but it was so real…"

"You need to relax and forget about all of your worries," Jenny ordered, standing from the arm of the couch. "Can you get out of an extra-curricular?"

"I could probably drop my afternoon tutoring writing songs," Lora reasoned. "I only have a few words down, but I like the theme of my new song."

"Then do it," her roommate smiled, stretching her arms above her head. "We could benefit from free afternoons and weekends this semester. How long is Jack here?"

"He has taken off for two weeks and saved all of his summer pay for the trip," Lora surmised. "He said he'd like to stay at least a life…"

"Perfect," Jenny smiled. "You can take him on weekend trip to Wacken Rockfest or the Lureberg… wherever you want really. Spend some time and enjoy. It'll do you some good."

"We could probably afford that," Lora drawled, thinking of the modest savings she had from her summer job as a free singer.

"Awesome," Jenny nodded, turning to her bag on the table. She pulled out her wallet, grabbed a handful of bills, and stuffed it back in her bag. "My father sent me a bonus allowance for the semester, but I won't need it all. Henry has offered to take me to Switzerland for Christmas, so I'm set. Take this for your trips with Jack."

"Oh, no," Lora said, shaking her head at her friend's outstretched fist of cash. "I couldn't take that from you, Jenny. I can barely afford my half of the rent and utilities."

"Nonsense," Jenny sighed, walking over and placing the cash in her hand. "It'll get you some decent plane tickets and a weekend somewhere nice. It is the least I can do."

"Thank you," Lora smiled, tearfully jumping to her feet and hugging her friend. "I don't deserve you."

"Oh, hush," Jenny chuckled, hugging her friend tightly. "You're fine. Besides, we're Rely – it means best friends. If I can't share my good fortune with you than what is the point of having money?"

The doorbell rang at that moment and Lora grinned, pulling a-way from her friend and grabbing the money from the counter for their food. After she grabbed the bags from the delivery boy and paid him, they both began to eat hungrily, laughing and enjoying a good bottle of wine with their noodles and rice. Lora loved her best friend like a sister and had always confided in her when she felt afraid or alone. After all, Jenny was the only person living that Lora had told her story to. She was the only person on this planet that knew about Lora's childhood nightmares and how vivid and dangerous they could become.

After their dinner, Jenny went to bed early, stating she had some homework to finish when in all reality, she was probably going to be talking to her current boyfriend, Henry. She'd been dating him since the semester started and since he was a rising rock star of the university's rock musicians, he was constantly on the road during the weekends to different concerts as pre-band. This didn't seem to bother her too much since she rarely lacked for companionship.

Lora had decided to tidy up her room before jumping into a re-laxing hot bath. She put her dirty laundry in a hamper, tidied up her bed, and made sure all her notes were in order so she could study them whenever she pleased. She also made sure to comb her hair before gathering her simple lace and linen nightgown into the bathroom. She undressed slowly, enjoying the cool water of the shower, scrubbing herself gently before washing out her long blonde hair. When she finally felt clean, she started drawing her-self a bath, content in the warmth of the bathroom now. It acted like a sauna, hot and full of steam as the tub filled.

She sat in that steaming tub of water for a while, allowing her muscles to fully relax as she lay there. It was the first time in a long time that she truly enjoyed a bath and she could feel the tension in her neck and shoulders fade away with the heat engulfing her. Her mind was truly at ease, thinking of only the relief she felt in that moment. Of course, the warmth surrounding her was also stimulating, recalling the last call she had with Jack last week about his planned flight.

He had told her what time he would be landing and then started to describe to her all the things he'd like to do when they met. Of course, Lora told him to wait until they could be alone in her apartment but the thought of being touched like that for the first time was a tantalizing one. She'd never been with a man and Jack was the only one she wanted. Getting to know him first as a friend, then as a lover, was something she looked forward to immensely.

She was still mulling over her relationship with Jack when she heard an odd noise coming from the living room. It sounded like Jenny was out of her room, walking around the apartment.

"Jenny?" Lora called, watching the door of the bathroom curiously. "I thought you were in..?"

There was no answer, so Lora got out of the bath, pulling the plug of the drain and dabbed herself dry with the fluffy white towel. Her hair was dripping so she started wrapping it in the towel on top of her head to dry it. She then slipped on her thin white gown and opened the door, the steam rushing out into the cooler hallway leading to the living room. Lora followed it, walking out to find that no one was there, the lights still on and the apartment door still latched and locked. She looked at Jenny's bedroom door and saw it was closed and her light was still on. Then, out of the corner of her eye she saw a puddle of water and then another.

She slowly started to realize they were wet footprints leading from the bathroom where she had just been toward the window of the living room. It was a massive window that overlooked the drive that was three stories down and the university which was only a couple of blocks to the north. However, the shades were drawn and that is where the footprints stopped. Lora looked at them curiously, then looked at her own drying feet, unsure what she was really seeing.

It was when she reached out to raise the curtain that she felt it. A shivering cold had crept up her spine creating goosebumps all over her legs and arms. She yanked on the string now, pulling the curtains back to reveal that outside the window wasn't the starlit sky and the rising moon beyond the horizon. It wasn't the typical canopies of changing trees and the lights of the university and city beyond spreading out before them. The scenery had changed entirely as if the entire building was submerged in water.

Outside the window crept large fish with glassy eyes and slack jaws. Among them were smaller schools of fish, swimming in the dark and frightening waters beyond. There arose large creatures, passing by the window like foreboding shadows intruding on her once safe home. She could hear the rush of water before she felt it, the clamoring thunderous rush of water as it sloshed over her feet and up her shins. The apartment was being flooded and soon the glass that held the horrifically dark and unknown world beyond would engulf her entire world.

She tried calling out for Jenny, but a loud crack rose above her voice, the window starting to shatter into hundreds of uneven lines and bolts of glass. She panicked, sloshing her way through knee-deep water toward the front door. She could feel the turning and sliding as the building seemed to sway with the unhindered violence of the water beyond the shattering window. It was like they were floating in the ebb and flow of the deep lake and soon, she would be sucked out into that dark abyss to await her unseen death.

She cried out again as water came rushing into the room from the front door, making her slide backward through the now waist-deep water. She managed to grab onto the kitchen counter, but it was made difficult as the entire building seemed to rotate. Down was up and up was down, and below her the water pooled on the glass of the window. She felt the fear take over her entire body, almost paralyzing her as her fingers desperately clung to the lip of the countertop. The water was rising and with a loud thud and a thunderous crack, the window below broke, letting the flood of water stream. She could feel it touching her toes now, wrenching her legs upright to try and cling closer to the countertop.

It was no use as the apartment around her entirely filled with water, her last breath too short as she struggled to remain anchored to the countertop. She was desperate for air, desperate to be out of these unknown depths where creatures waited for her to finally lose consciousness. Then, she spotted a sight that paralyzed her where she clung. Deep within the depths, staring up at her with glowing eyes was a creature. It watched her every move and Lora could feel it's gaze as she clung there, refusing to look back down at the frightening sight that awaited her.

Then, she let out a yelp, the last of her breath lost as cold painful water rushed into her mouth, causing her to lose her grip on her anchor. She drifted helplessly, clinging at her throat and kicking as she sunk deeper, beyond the broken window and into the depths of the black-eyed monster's clutches. She kicked and screamed, felt the water rushing into her mouth and lungs as she clung to life and tried to push her way to the surface. It was then that she felt it, a sharp piercing hook in her left shoulder that clung heavily, dragging her swiftly into the depths.

She saw it, a gnarled hooked claw that dug into her shoulder deeply as she was drug further down. She could feel her throat burning, her nose rushing with the same burning sensation as the pale claw grasped at her. Blood pooled and rushed by her as she sunk, her ears popping and her body thrashing in pain as she drew closer and closer to those black eyes below. That pale scaly claw that hooked her like a fish was grimy and covered in barnacles and horrible deformities that pulsed and scratched her as she started to lose consciousness. Everything was fading, the water rushing past her, her ears popping loudly and painfully as the strangulation of cold water clasped her throat like a vice. She was dead, she knew it, and she only hoped she died before she reached the jaws of this massive and unforgiving creature in the depths.

Lora raised her head with a scream, finding herself in the bathtub. She ignored the warm blood running down her spine and the chill that overtook her as she realized it was just a dream. She was breathing unevenly, trying to calm herself but the fear and cold had overtaken her and she was shaking erratically. She ran to the bedroom and collapsed sideways onto the bed now, feeling light-theaded. Lora was desperate to catch her breath and as she lay there, deeply inhaling the sharp cold air.

She felt the burning in her throat slowly start to subside and could clearly see the dark room around her come into focus. She was taking deep breaths through her nose, exhaling through her mouth as she tried to calm herself. Once the adrenaline had subsided, and the sweating had stopped, her body had started to regain function. She was able to stretch her legs out and her body had stopped shivering. When it seemed like everything was calming down, she realized her shoulder was stinging and burning and she slowly raised her hand to figure out what was going on.

She felt the sticky warm substance on her shoulder and froze, feeling the burning sensation intensify. She lay there motionless, trying to understand what had happened, wondering how her dream could have had real-world implications. She must have done it unconsciously, scratching herself in her terrible nightmare. She slowly began to move now, placing her feet on the floor and lifting herself shakily from the bed. She wandered from her bedroom across the hall to the bathroom, turning on the light to see that she was frighteningly pale, sickly looking, and blood had stained the strap of her dress and her shoulder. There, a long cut was shining scarlet across her shoulder and down her back, her eyes straining to see all of it in the mirror behind her.

She started to shiver again but steeled herself, slipping off the garment and grabbing the medical supplies from the cabinet. After twenty minutes of trying to patch and clean the wound, she was able to dress it and switch to a different long t-shirt to sleep in. She was still shaken as she switched the light back off and went back to her bed. She didn't bother looking at the clock, lying on her opposite side and staring at the door of her room thoughtlessly, fighting sleep with everything in her. She feared the nightmares from her childhood had returned and she only hoped that she could find a way to overcome them before it got out of hand.

She lay there in bed, staring at her door until the bright beams of sunlight peaked over the horizon through her blinds. She didn't know how long she had laid there but the pain in her shoulder had only dulled as she watched the room lighten into day. The sounds of life outside her window woke Jenny who sauntered into the bathroom unaware that her roommate was laying, fearfully paralyzed, on her bed just on the other side of the wall.

Eventually, Lora got out of bed, looking at her phone and realizing it was almost noon. Jack had texted her and she hadn't even acknowledged it, setting her phone back down and sauntering out of her room. She didn't expect to see Jenny cleaning, something delicious cooking on the stovetop. Lora eyed her curiously, her roommate oblivious to the fact that she was being watched. She was busy mixing the new soundtrack on her laptop.

Lora just grinned, turning from the living room to the bathroom, cautiously glancing at the window. It wasn't cracked, wasn't abnormally broken, and overlooked the familiar campus and river beyond. She sighed in relief, going into the bathroom to look at her bandage and change it. She pulled it off, noting the little bit of blood that had stained it before redressing the wound. When she was done, she got dressed, throwing on a pair of shorts and a t-shirt before emerging back into the living room. By then, Jenny was done sound mixing, checking the food on the stove in the kitchen.

"I see you're finally awake," she drawled, grinning at Lora. "Up late texting Jack?"

"Not really," Lora sighed, sitting down slowly on the couch. "It was a long night."

"Didn't sleep at all?" Jenny asked, putting the lid back on the pan and moving into the living room. "What's wrong?"

"I didn't get a lot of sleep," Lora admitted, leaning back against the couch slowly. "It's nothing… like you said, I need to relax."

"You're so wound up," Jenny said, lounging next to Lora on the couch. "What's going on, huh? What's got you stressed out?"

"I don't know," Lora admitted, sighing loudly. "I just don't understand. Everything is going great, there is nothing to stress about and yet I'm on edge."

"Is it our new song, or is it Jack? Are you nervous about meeting him?"

"No," Lora said, shaking her head. "I want to meet him, I want to be with him. I don't have any fears when it comes to our song. Maybe that is it? I'm so confident and happy about us that I fear something must go wrong. Nothing can be this good?"

"Now you're just creating your own problems," Jenny reasoned, placing her arm over Lora's shoulder. She winced and Jenny immediately noticed, searching her for the injury. When she spotted the large bandage of gauze and tape, her brow knitted in confusion.

"It's nothing," Lora said, looking up at her friend sheepishly. "I just hurt myself is all."

"That's all?" Jenny asked, moving to see just how bad the injury was. She stood up, leaped over the back of the couch and lifted Lora's shirt. She saw that it went across her left shoulder and down her back and she groaned, inspecting it closely. "You need to clean this better. Come on, let's go to the bathroom."

"I don't really know how I did it," Lora confessed, feeling guilty. "I woke up and it was there."

"You could have done it to yourself unknowingly," Jenny suggested, setting her friend down on the closed toilet seat as she addressed the bandage. She took it off slowly, both girls silent as the wound was cleaned properly and dressed with a decent bandage. Once she was done, she cleaned up, helping Lora back to the living room slowly.

"Just relax," Jenny instructed, going back to the kitchen to check on her food. She stirred it, shut off the pot, and moved it to another burner before returning to the living room to sit across from Lora on one of the armchairs. "So, tell me what happened."

"I took a shower and bath before bed, I had a nightmare, and I woke up with this cut on my shoulder," Lora explained, unsure how to make it sound believable. "I don't know how the cut happened, but it did, and I stayed awake all night trying to figure out how."

"What was the dream about?"

"I was drowning," Lora whispered, remembering the terror that had paralyzed her. "I was in our apartment when it became submerged in water. There was a horrific creature lurking in the depths and it got me, dragging me down. I was so afraid and when I woke, I was drenched in blood and shivering from head to toe."

"It was just like the other visions, wasn't it?" Jenny asked, leaning forward to take Lora's hands.

"More intense," she replied, feeling sleepy. "More ferocious and real, like I was actually drowning in this deep water. There was a claw in my shoulder, right where my wound is at and I just don't know how it happened. I don't know if I'm hurting myself or if it's just a coincidence. It frightens me…"

"Breathe," Jenny encouraged, placing a hand on Lora's head. "It could be some sort of trauma working its way to the surface or an untreated illness. I don't know but I think you should arrange an appointment with a psychologist. I know a few great ones here in the city that could help you, if you chose to go."

"You think it could be a mental illness?" Lora asked, fearful of what that could mean. "I don't know much about my family, but that kind of thing runs in the family, right?"

"Not always," Jenny smiled, nodding encouragingly. "But we can find out together."

"I'll make an appointment later today," Lora nodded, agreeing that something had to be done about these horror visions. They had vanished for so long when she lived with her aunt but now, they had resurfaced just like when her aunt had passed. It was something she couldn't fathom and knew that something had to be done about it. She didn't want to hurt herself.

"Go, lay down," Jenny offered, standing to help her to bed. "I'll keep watch on you and I'll keep the food warm in case you wake with an appetite, alright?"

"Thank you," Lora smiled, taking her friend's arm. "I don't know what I would do without you."

"You'd be fine," she chuckled, leading her into her bedroom. "You're smart and resourceful. You'll do fine but for now, you need me to look after you. Don't worry, I'll be diligent."

"I wish I had a sister like you," Lora smiled, sitting slowly on her bed.

"I am your sister, you idiot," Jenny smirked, helping her to lay down in bed as she covered her friend with her blanket. "I'll turn on some soothing music, okay?"

"Thanks," Lora smiled, snuggling deeply against her pillow and comforter. "Please, wake me in a couple of hours. I don't want to be up all night again."

"Will do," Jenny smiled, leaving the door propped open as she disappeared back into the living room. Soon there was relaxing instrumental music wafting through the air and it made Lora yawn. She was ready to nap and forget her horrible vision and fears. She knew that there was truly nothing to fear and that soon, she could get the help she needed to avoid the progression of these horrific visions.

Rock Dream

"Organization of sound in time produces a wonderful art we call Music. To some… music is life. To others music is happiness…Music conveys different feelings according to the pattern of sound…" staring ahead, Lora listened attentively to every single word with interest. Everything made sense; the strumming of her guitar alongside the sound from her voice was something she found sacred. Lora didn't just like music, but the creativity behind it, the artistry that granted her an exchange year in Germany from Portland, USA.

"I asked for permission to use the studio and it was granted, but we need some money to pay the crew," Lora said, placing her notebook in her bag before raising her head to look at Jenny, standing beside the seat wearing a white shirt and black short shorts complimenting knee-high boots.

"Yes, gonna record" She squealed, jumping around, causing her long black hair with streaks of red in the front to bounce, ignoring the stares from people around. Lora chuckled and pulled a happy Jenny out of the hall. "Wait! for how long?"Jenny asked, suddenly stopping in her tracks as they walked through the corridor.

"For as long as we need to finish the song. Jimmy, the organizer of the rock battle said he found our new song entertaining and sees potential," Lora said a huge smile of her cheeks.

"Make way for the new Clash," Jenny shouted, lifting up her hands with a peace sign, before sticking her tongue out. Lora's smile widened and she also lifted her hands as they ran to their rehearsal cellar room. The rehearsal room was spacious with bare walls of dark brown bricks. Everywhere stood equipment, different e-guittars, electric drum set and a dark graffiti showing two mangas in gothic style with the band name RELY, decorating the corner beside the only metal window.

Jenny sat down at the drum set, turned to Lora and started singing. "Now the King told the boogie man." Jenny sang, hitting hard on the drums in accordance with the beat.

"You have to let the ragae drop." Lora continued, bopping her head. They began to sing together, both bopping their heads.

"Rockin' the Casbah," Jenny shouted the chorus, fully immerse in the rhythm. They came into their rehearsal room.

Jenny and Lora have been spending most of their time in the rehearsing room. They have had whole new adventures in this room, so they loved being there. Their guitars were flaming from the cool beats they have been playing. The room was dark, only the laptop's screen brightening it. Also, the instruments had little red and green lights. The room was very comfortable and cozy. When Lora was stepping in she felt that specific music smell: sex smell mixed with the smell of fire. Also, the poster of RELY was perfecting everything in the room.

Once when they were rehearsing in the room Jenny started playing a new beat she had mastered for the upcoming rock battle.

"Jenny it's very cool, this beat is too cool for people like me having only five fingers! For this speed, it would be better to have two more fingers on the left and one more on the right hand."

Jenny answered, "Yea babe, it's a new piece, it's still a work in progress, I mean to change the beat to the mid a little, I guess."

Lora looked at her "Yep, I like it but I need more time."

"We have a lot of time, "Jenny said, "It's our job to have time, we are music students."

Lora placed her hand to a new cord "Some, some, rock band sadness, we don't care, we assume the meaning of the professors, we don't apologize having no time, we don't start changing on our lyrics, and to the end its some punk-rock music left."

Jenny added a monotone bass guitar cords in "Yeah, real?"

Lora answered singing, "Yeah, punk rock"

Jenny leans back, "Yeahs babe am punk rock musician, I don't have spent time to rehearse, I don't have record sessions, I don't need youtube, I just piss off, I like it."

Jenny exhausted, wraping the instrument in.

Lora took a sip from the water bottle "I like when you have this mental spark."

Jenny don't smile anymore triyng to concentrate "It's much more, I see it coming."

Lora starts playing guitar according to improv lyrics "Rely on the stage, the hearts is the wave,"

Jenny follows, "It's inside of us, it's a drowned star."

Lora changed her voice, "We follow the call, we open the hearts."

Jenny turned to Lora like a lesbian having some romance moment, "Be relaxed, I like your tongue, your hands, your ever first song, and I will change the beat tonight for our first record session tomorrow, it gonna be great."

Lora surprised "What? You cheat, you got us record?"

Both overly happy, Lora took Jenny in a hug and they both start jumping up and down. This was the moment Lora has always been dreaming of.

Jenny screams of the happiness "We got two record session for two days, babe, and after recording, we can rock battle with finalists. If we had uploaded our session on youtube."

They were suddenly interrupted by a ring tone and Lora quickly placed her hand in her pocket, feeling the vibration. Her smile widened when she saw the caller Id. #honey

"Hello, babe." She said in a sing-song voice.

"Hi." She heard the deep voice of her boyfriend Jake. "Guess who's coming to visit?" Jake said, joy evident in his voice.

"Did it work, can you come?" She squealed, raising her eyes to watch Jenny get up from the stool, gently placing the drumsticks on them.

"Yes, and I bought tickets for the Rock festival at Loreley, I heard my girlfriend is performing there," Jake said, with a very serious note in his voice.

"Yep," Lora squealed again, walking to the wall to gently place the guitar down. She gasped after her eyes landed on her wristwatch.

"Sorry babe, I have my next lecture in two minutes," she said. "See you soon, hate you."

"I hope so, hate you more." Jack chuckled and hung up.

"Whatever rock festival that is, we have to finish the song first, then win the battle, then I'm coming with you on the big stage," Jenny said, leaning on the wall beside the RELY wall art.

"How did you hear that?" Lora asked, looking at her in confusion while picking up her bag.

"It's one of my many superpowers," Jenny said and Lora chuckled before they both headed out the door.

Lora was awoken by a buzzing, her phone still sitting on her bedside table as she left it earlier that morning. She took it in her hand lazily, yawning as she unlocked it to read the message from her boyfriend.

Jack: I haven't heard from you all day. Are you alright?

Lora: I'm fine, just tired. The semester has been busy so far but I am dropping my recording sessions in the afternoon and on weekends. That will give us more time together. I can't wait to see you.

Jack: I cannot wait to see you either. I want to spend every second with you. My girls have given me an early birthday present! An extra $500 for my trip.

Lora: That is fantastic! We'll see Europe together. I cannot wait to have you in my arms. I have been thinking about nothing else.

Jack: I have been waiting to hold you in my arms for years. What is a couple more weeks, sweet baby?

Lora: I had a bad vision. I want to be with you so badly. I wish you could be here right now.

Jack: Two more days. Wait and be excited. When I get there, it will be gone.

Lora: I cannot wait. Think about me until then.

Jack: I will and when I see you, I won't hesitate to show you exactly how much I've been thinking about you.

Lora: When we get back to my place, I will show you everything. Follow your own advice, my love. Be patient.

Jack: Tease.

Lora: Goodnight, Jack.

Jack: Good evening my love.

Lora rose from her bed now, stretching slowly as she noticed how low the sun had gotten. She must have slept for nearly three hours, smiling at the delicious aroma of food from the kitchen beyond. She quickly sauntered from her room to the kitchen, noting the delectable dishes Jenny was plating up.

"Looks like someone had a good nap," Jenny commented, putting the final garnish on her fish. "What would you like? I made a buffet of tasty dishes."

"A little of everything," she nodded, moving around the counter to grab a plate. "I'm starving."

"Good," Jenny nodded, scooping little bits of food, small fish, potato and cabbage dishes on her plate before seating her at the counter. Lora excitedly seated herself on the stool, hungrily digging into the feast. Jenny only giggled, pouring her roommate a glass of wine.

"This is amazing," Lora nodded, taking the glass from her friend. "Sleep and a little relaxation are exactly what I needed."

"I'm glad to hear that," Jenny nodded, picking at some of the food and putting it on her own plate. Once she was satisfied with the food she chose, she sat down next to Lora, smiling nervously.

"What?" Lora asked, unsure what her friend was up to.

"I got the number for my friend, the psychologist," Jenny admitted, unsure how Lora would react. "She said she can fit you in tomorrow afternoon if you're willing."

Lora contemplated this for a moment, remembering the fear she had felt that morning from the vision and how it had completely drained her. She was also worried that she was unknowingly hurting herself. She knew it wasn't normal and that professional help could be the answer. She also knew that Jenny expected her to follow through with her plans from earlier to call the doctor herself.

"Alright, I can do that," Lora finally nodded, taking a bite from her plate. "I'll go see what she has to say. Maybe it is all just in my mind and it is something she can shed some light on."

"I'm really glad to hear that you'll go," Jenny smiled, raising her own cup of wine at her friend. "If anything, it could just be the stress of school and your past trauma catching up with you. Nothing can be overlooked when it comes to your mental stability."

"True," Lora nodded, raising her own glass. "To mental stability."

"To mental stability," Jenny smiled, clinking her glass against Lora's and drinking the cup in one gulp.

"So, who is this psychiatrist, if you don't mind me asking?"

"Oh," Jenny smiled, setting her cup down. "Her name is Ursula and she's a friend of my fathers. I think that they used to sleep together. She's only seven years older than I am and my father helped her found her practice last year."

"Is she any good?" Lora questioned, feeling skeptical.

"Very," Jenny smiled. "She is fully licensed with clients like a-list executives and state leaders. I'm not supposed to know that, but she is very good at her job."

"If you think she'll help, I'll give it a try, but I hope she takes government insurance," Lora mused, looking at her friend. "I can't afford some outrageous price like most psychiatrists charge."

"She'll consider it a favor for a friend," Jenny assured, taking a bite of her food. "Don't worry, everything is settled."

"What time tomorrow?" Lora asked, munching on her own meal slowly.

"14:00," Jenny smiled, pouring herself more wine. "Just be there and see what she has to say. If she can help you, it is worth a try."

"True, but I hope Jack never finds out," Lora replied, feeling slightly apprehensive now. "No one wants to date someone who needs to see a psychiatrist."

"That's not true," Jenny affirmed, shaking her head. "Almost all successful people see psychiatrists. It is a way to fully explore your emotions and fears to try and overcome what holds you back. It is really empowering."

"You seem passionate about all this," Lora smirked, munching on the delicious rolls Jenny made. "Why don't you study psychology?"

"Of course I do," Jenny shrugged. "Besides, if I want to move up as a rock star, with more inner energy, I need to learn hard."

"Valid point," Lora nodded, munching happily on the hearty meal. She was so stuffed when she was done, she felt sleepy, both she and Jenny cuddling up on their large couch together to watch a movie before passing out from the slow and relaxing day that they had had. It was in times like this that Lora truly appreciated her close relationship with Jenny. She truly would be lost without her best friend.

Lora sat uncomfortably in the waiting room of the office, Jenny smiling serenely at her as they waited for her appointment. The fountain near the doorway and the soft nature music playing through the speakers above them was quite relaxing. It was when someone emerged from the doctor's office that Lora started feeling even more nervous. Jenny realized that and smiled, taking her friend's hand gently.

"It is okay," Jenny explained. "You talk about whatever you like with her, okay? Nothing is forbidden and she will try to help you. I'll be right out here, waiting, okay?"

"Yeah," Lora nodded, watching the door nervously. The secretary, a young woman with fair hair and deep green eyes was talking on the phone now, glancing in Lora and Jenny's direction before hanging up the phone. She then stood from her desk, walking over to them with a kind smile.

"The Doctor will see you now," she said, motioning for them to follow her. Jenny stood, motioning for Lora to go first before they entered the adjoining room. It was a much cozier atmosphere; the wood finishing and bookshelves added a regal touch to the office. The plush lounger and wing-backed chairs near a solid wooden desk made it seem like this should have been the office of some rich old patriarch, not a young woman.

"Ah, Jenny," came an unfamiliar voice and Lora turned to see a young woman in a fashionable pantsuit, a genuine smile on her face. She embraced Jenny gently, kissing her on the cheek before pulling away with a nod. "How have you been?"

"Good," Jenny confirmed, placing a hand on Lora's shoulder. "This is my roommate, Lora."

"Nice to meet you, Lora," Ursula smiled, offering her hand. Lora took it gratefully, shaking it before turning back to the room.

"It has been a while," Jenny affirmed, looking about the office as well. "Spared no expense, did you?"

"Not at all," she smiled, offering them each some tea. After she was situated in her chair, she turned to Lora, a curious twinkle in her eye. "So, Lora, what brings you here today?"

"I… I don't really know what to say," Lora explained, glancing at Jenny as they both sat down on the lounge chair.

"If you'd prefer, we can make this a private session," Ursula offered, Jenny immediately setting down her tea and standing up. "Will you wait outside, Jenny?"

"No problem at all," she nodded, picking the tea up again. "But I'm taking this with me."

The three of them chuckled and Jenny left the room, shutting the door behind her with a snap. Lora immediately felt awkward, unsure how to even begin such a conversation with a complete stranger. However, Ursula seemed completely at ease, sipping her tea slowly as she watched Lora.

"You are aware that I cannot speak to anyone about what we discuss here," Ursula drawled, smiling over her cup. "You can tell me anything and I am legally bound to keep it to myself."

"Unless I've murdered someone," Lora corrected, making Ursula grimace at her. "I haven't, by the way."

"Humor is a great way to defuse tension but is there a reason for the tension in the first place?"

"I'm not used to laying out my problems to strangers, let alone professional psychiatrists," Lora confessed, feeling a bit uncertain about all of this. "This was probably a mistake…"

"There must be a reason you came in today," Ursula reasoned. "So, what is it? What do you want to say? Sometimes all it takes is a few words and suddenly, a river of words comes pouring out."

"I've been having horror visions," Lora confessed, feeling compelled to just get this all over with. "I used to have them as a child and when my parents died, they got worse. When I lived with my aunt, they started to subside but when she passed away only a couple years ago, they briefly returned. When I was a child, I used to scratch myself, fall out of bed, or sleepwalk but I haven't done that since I was nine. Now, suddenly, the vivid dreams of monstrous creatures and a deep abyss have returned and this time, I ended up hurting myself quite badly."

"I don't know what to believe," Lora continued, unable to stop herself from working this problem out with Ursula. "I don't know if I am subconsciously doing this to myself or if I am hallucinating. I don't know if anything is real, but it feels real because, in the vision, I was attacked by a ghost underwater, I was bitten by my left shoulder. That is where I was hurt, and it just doesn't make any sense to me."

"My dreams never have," she whispered, feeling panic set in. "They used to be just as horrible as a child, my mother's soothing touch the only thing that could get rid of my fears. Now, I don't know what to do and I freeze up, unable to stop the panic and shock that sets in. Is this something from my past resurfacing? What does any of it mean? It just frightens me, and I feel like it is going to cause me to really lose my sanity and hurt myself or the ones I love."

They both sat quietly for a moment, Ursula seeming to evaluate the situation more closely as her deep eyes never left Lora's face. Even as she frantically spoke about her fear and the dreams that plagued her, Ursula kept an open and relaxed expression, never once giving away her thoughts. When Lora finished, she looked even more serene, analyzing everything about Lora at that moment like she was some sort of test rat.

"You're afraid of losing your mind to whatever it is that haunts your visions," Ursula reasoned, watching Lora as she sipped her tea again. "This is natural, especially when you are self-inflicting wounds as a result of these vivid dreams. It could be a bacterial or viral infection making you hallucinate so I would highly recommend going to a doctor to see if there is any changes or problems. However, from what little I can tell from your body language and mannerisms, you seem to be a very uptight and perhaps high-strung person."

"You are constantly trying to solve problems and make yourself busy," Ursula affirmed, setting her cup down. "This isn't a bad thing because in doing so you keep yourself healthy and happy in your relationships with other people. However, it becomes problematic when the body and mind are continuously in motion. My recommendation would be to relax, have good sex, find your balance and maintain it."

"Relax?" Lora questioned, skeptically staring at the woman. "You don't understand, it isn't because I am wound up. It has to be more complicated than that."

"Most people want to analyze and come up with a reason why there is something wrong," Ursula admitted, watching Lora seriously. "They invent problems, manifesting what they consider to be more problems. However, most of it is all in our head. We believe there is no escaping this cycle and that something must go bad in order for something good to happen. That is where you are at right now."

"You believe you are at the zenith of the wheel and the only direction you can go from there is down," Ursula concluded, smiling at Lora. "You may be right, and it may be an acute mental breakdown due to past trauma or stress. However, I would like to explore more before we come to any definitive conclusions. Would you be willing to make an appointment with your family physician? I can write a recommendation for them to consider. I won't know more until that time."

"There is something wrong with me," Lora affirmed, knowing that it wasn't normal to feel this way. It wasn't normal, her real-world switches to hell, nor was it normal to wake up with large gashes in your shoulder that match the wounds from your nightmare. Something didn't add up and Ursula wasn't helping shed any light on the situation.

"So far, I find nothing out of the ordinary about you except for some paranoia and distress," Ursula admitted, watching her. "But you truly believe there is something wrong?"

"Yes!" Lora admitted, allowing some of her frustration to show. "I know there is. You don't dream about being drowned into the deep, encountering demons and suffering real-world wounds from such a dream. It is just impossible."

"With demons," Ursula surmised. "Real demons or emotional ones from past trauma and experiences?"

"Real ones," Lora sighed, unsure how to make herself any clearer. "I used to have similar dreams as a child, hurting myself and waking from terrible hallucinations. I was never treated with medication because the dreams soon disappeared. They resurfaced last night. I'm telling you, there is more to all of this than just stress."

"You have courage, and it's a good sign. I'd like you to go to your doctor, get a physical with my recommendation, and then come back for another session," Ursula encouraged, writing something down on a nearby notepad. "Come back Tuesday with your results, okay?"

"I can't afford to pay for sessions with you," Lora admitted, feeling ashamed. "I'm sorry but I just can't afford it. I know I need psychiatric help, but the expense is too much."

"I'll take on your case for free," Ursula nodded, handing her the piece of paper from her notepad. "Just please, come back. I think there are some issues in your past that we can work out and I know that you know that. Otherwise, you wouldn't be here asking for help."

"I'll consider it," Lora nodded, standing from the couch. "But I don't see how talking about it can stop me from harming myself. Thanks for your time."

"A pleasure," Ursula nodded, standing and taking Lora's hand. "But please, come back Tuesday at the same time. I am sure that if your family doctor cannot find the problem, I can."

"Thanks," Lora nodded, shaking her hand before turning to leave. Once she was back out into the reception area, Jenny stood up, curiously eyeing her friend.

"That didn't take very long," she nodded, looking back at the door. "What did she say?"

"She said I should go to my family doctor, get a physical on her recommendation, and return Tuesday to go over the results," Lora explained, looking hesitantly at the note in her hand. "I don't think she understands what is really going on."

"Give her a chance," Jenny encouraged. "Go to the doctor, get the results, and come back Tuesday. I hope she can explain the problem, even if it is just a mild panic attack or some sort of trauma."

"Fine," Lora nodded, glancing at the receptionist briefly before leading her friend back toward the large oak door that was the entrance to the office. "I'll go but I'm really hoping she gives me some meds or something to help me sleep."

"Set up an appointment with your doctor tomorrow," Jenny encouraged, unlocking the car with her key. "We'll see what they say and take it from there, okay?"

"Sounds good," Lora smiled, opening the door to Jenny's fashionable Cabrio. "I'll call once we leave. I really hope they have some open availability sometime tomorrow. I can't imagine waiting another day like this. It's almost unbearable."

Ursula recommended they meet two times a week for short sessions in which Lora would talk about her past and her dreams. She'd revealed many intimate details about her family and childhood to Ursula and felt like she was more than just a psychiatrist, but a friend.

She also found that her own need to be perfect and to organize her life based on what she wanted for her future only caused more tension between her past and present. It was like she was compartmentalizing all her problems and trying to organize them so that she might one day come back to them. She kept herself busy though, not willing to look back on painful memories that only sharpened with time. This was what Ursula tried to get her to see and she understood this inherent weakness that brought her nothing but trouble.

It was in her next session, that she had made a real breakthrough. Ursula had explained to her that her life wasn't just a random set of events that she couldn't control but a story she had to write. It was something quite poetic that encouraged Lora to admit that she had always feared her dreams. She'd never understood why but even when she was a child, her mother would tell her old stories about how dreams could open the doorway to the other world.

"Do you think she meant literal doorways?" Ursula asked, pouring Lora some more tea. "Or was she speaking figuratively, like creatively?"

"She was so serious," Lora recalled, her aunt having similar traits. "It was like she was teaching me a lesson when she told me those stories about ghosts and other creatures that lurked in the dark worlds within rivers and oceans."

"So, this could be a deeply held religious or philosophical belief your family has held," Ursula reasoned, smiling over her cup. "Do you think your visions are your psyche reliving the trauma of losing your family at such a young age?"

"I've always had to rely on myself," Lora shrugged, sipping her own hot cup of tea and lemon. "In school, when I could finally work summer jobs, and even when I lived with my aunt. She wasn't a very sociable woman."

"So, do you think this is your mind's way of rebelling against that constant tension between your past and how you lead your life now?"

"Honestly, I feel like my visions were always a curse," Lora admitted, feeling a little ashamed. "It was always something that was with me, as a child and even beyond. I always feared their return and when they did finally resurface, I had to find something to justify their existence. I didn't know that by trying to reason with logic, I had given them such power over me."

"And now?"

"Something has slid into place," Lora affirmed, setting down her cup. "I feel like everything makes sense now and that in order for me to accept the loss of my family, I had to focus my fear and anxiety on something that I thought was out of my control. These sessions have helped me to realize that it isn't what is out of my control that frightens me. It is the excessive control of my own life that has led me to relive these events and their trauma in my dreams."

"And so, you've unlocked the secret," Ursula smiled, nodding slowly. "You've taken the first steps by identifying what has caused such anxiety and pain in your life and accepting them as a part of you. You should be proud. Most people never reach this critical juncture."

"Thank you," Lora smiled, checking the time on her phone. "And with that, I should be off. Jack lands in an hour and I want to make sure I am there early enough to meet him at his gate."

"Have fun," Ursula nodded, standing from her chair. Lora nodded, gathering her things into her purse before leaving the office, waving goodbye to her one more time.

She hardly realized how excited she was until she pulled into the parking garage at the airport, her hands shaking as the adrenaline started to kick in. His plane would be landing in a little over a half an hour and she wanted to hurry through security so she could meet him as he stepped off the plane. She felt nervous the whole way through security, noting the looks from the guards as she slipped out of her heals and placed them on the belt to go through the scanner along with her purse. She also stood in the machine, spreading her legs and arms out as she waited for approval to leave the line.

Once through the checkpoint, shoes back on and bag slung over her shoulder, she quickly walked toward his gate. It wasn't far, half-way down the main terminal. She could see the plane landing, the wheels touching down on the tarmac as she arrived at Gate Four. She waited, impatiently watching out the window as the white and blue plane rolled up slowly to the gate. She watched as the causeway rolled toward the plane and in that moment, she felt fear take hold.

She wasn't sure why she felt like this, but it was almost paralyzing as she stood, hesitantly, by the window overlooking the huge runway. She wondered if he'd recognize her. Jenny had convinced her to wear the tight sommer dress that showed off her curves, her arms wrapped tightly around her torso to try and hide them from other travelers who were keenly aware of her prescience.

She never considered herself beautiful and had always felt like her looks were average. She wasn't particularly tall, but she had fair ivory skin with small brown freckles dotting her shoulders and arms. She had fair golden hair with deep blue eyes and she hardly considered herself to be desirable but the looks from passing travelers, particularly men, made her keenly aware of how seductive she must have looked that day. It didn't help that her blonde curly locks were wild about her as she stood there, waiting for the man she'd yearned to meet.

The announcement of his plane's arrival only made her more nervous, as the doors opened to allow passengers to exit into the terminal. She waited, watching for him to appear. When she finally saw him, emerging into the terminal wide-eyed and curious, she felt herself drawn to him. It didn't take him long to recognize her in the crowd, his smile widening as he set his backpack and messenger bag down at his feet. She almost ran into his arms, feeling them tighten around her as his lips found hers.

It was a passionate kiss, neither of them noticing the groups of tourists and passengers walking by them with curious or disapproving glares. Lora didn't care, loving the feel of his arms around her as they embraced. She wanted to stay like this forever, her face pressed against the crook of his neck as he held her against him. It was almost too perfect and before long, they realized that they were the only ones left at the gate. Lora only giggled, pulling back to look up at his face.

Jenny was right – Jack was strikingly handsome. His green eyes found hers immediately and were alight with excitement and anticipation. He looked somewhat tired but that didn't diminish the fire that blazed behind his dusky orbs. His wide grin and mischievous chuckle made her heart melt as he captured her lips with his again. When they finally pulled apart, Jack chuckled, holding her at arm's length to take in her outfit.

"Wow," he breathed, his accent still thick and somewhat comical. "You look amazing."

"So do you," she mused, placing a hand on his chest. "I've been waiting for you for so long. It seems like a lifetime."

"So," he smiled, stepping closer and wrapping his arms around her waist. "This was Nazi Germany, and now your study country?"

"This is it," she chuckled, motioning around. "I hope you enjoy it while you are here."

"As long as I am with you," he whispered, pressing her closer to him as he kissed her neck. "I've wanted to hold you like this. I still can't believe this is happening."

"Come on," she encouraged, taking his hand and pulling him away. "I'll drive you to my campus."

He only nodded, picking up his small backpack and satchel before following her through the now empty terminal. Once they emerged onto the causeway that led the parking garage, Jack sighed in relief.

"It was not that easy to leave my green girls," he smiled at her, squeezing her hand gently. "but I'm so glad to be here."

"You mean your water plants," she whispered, blushing slightly. "I hate them, but now I know you love me more than them…"

"I cannot wait to hear your new song," he smirked, wrapping his arm around her waist as they walked toward the garage. "Will I get to meet the famous Jenny?"

"She's out for the evening," Lora smirked, making him unconsciously lick his lips. "It's just you and I tonight, Jack."

"Perfect," he whispered, leaning down to kiss her just below her ear. "I've wanted to be alone with you for a very, very long time."

"I look forward to it," she assured, pushing the button to unlock her car as they approached.

The ride back into the city and campus was torture, almost an hour of tension as the couple talked about random landmarks, differences between the two countries, and the plans they might make in the days to come. However, hanging between them was a palpable sexual arousal that had entranced them, making the trip from the airport that much more unbearable. Whenever Jack reached over to graze her bare knee or caress her neck, she could feel the goosebumps arise, the need to have him close overpowering all thought. He must have felt the same way, his eyes glazing over and deepening as he took in her every curve.

Lora could feel the urge to have him there in her car, somewhere in an alleyway or abandoned parking lot, overpowering her good senses. She had never wanted so desperately to be with him alone and the thought of what he could do to her only increased the tension between them. She only hoped that Jenny was already gone by the time they got to the apartment. She claimed she was leaving that afternoon, but Lora was unsure if she had already left for Henry's apartment that night. Lora desperately hoped they'd be a-lone and prayed her best friend and roommate had anticipated her wishes.

Lora unlocked the deadbolt to her apartment, feeling Jack's presence just behind her as she did so. There was something erotic about him standing behind her, almost pinning her to the door as she struggled to open it. It was instinctual, the way she pressed against him as they both stood in the hallway, desperate to be on the other side of the door.

When the lock finally clicked, Lora stepped in, standing aside so Jack could come in. Neither of them expected to see Jenny loun-ging on the couch in the living room. She smiled simply up at the couple and then stood up, introducing herself to Jack.

"Nice to meet you finally," she said, offering her hand. "I'm Jenny."

"The Jenny," he mused, smiling down at Lora. "I've heard so much about you."

"Likewise," Jenny nodded, shaking his hand. "So, what are you kids up to tonight?"

Lora almost kicked her friend, shaking her head at her sugges-tion before motioning to her bedroom door just down the short hallway.

"You can put your things in there," she smiled, stealing a kiss from him as he passed to put away his things. When he was out of sight, Lora rounded on Jenny, unsure why her friend was still lin-gering around.

"I had to check him out," Jenny admitted, shrugging her shoul-ders. "I needed to make sure you were in good hands. He is very handsome; good job."

"You're impossible," Lora smirked, waving at her friend to leave. "Don't care, I'll text you in the morning."

"Be safe," Jenny motioned, looking down the hallway at Lora's open bedroom door. "There are some gums in my room if you need them."

"Thanks," Lora blushed, motioning for Jenny to leave. "Now go."

"Don't drink all the good wine," Jenny warned, grabbing her jacket from the closet near the front door. "And don't disturb the neighbors."

"Just go," Lora pleaded, desperately trying to hurry her friend out the door.

"Have fun," Jenny offered, slipping on her shoes and grabbing her keys. "See you in the morning. Don't forget the recording session."

And with that, Jenny left, snapping the door shut behind her with a chuckle as her friend locked it from within. Lora then started tidying up, frantically kicking off her heels and straightening up the living room and counter again. She had done the same thing that morning, unsure if it was tidy enough for Jack. He was never really picky about organization, but she wanted to make a good first impression.

When he emerged from her bedroom, Lora smiled, leaning lazily against the back of the couch. He didn't waste any time, coming over and wrapping her in his arms possessively.

"You look so good," he whispered, his lips grazing her neck as his hot breath caressed her skin. "Better than I could have ever dreamed about."

"So do you," she replied, her voice soft and hesitant. "You were so worried, but I don't know why."

"You think so?" he asked, trailing kisses from her jaw down her neck to her exposed collarbone. "I always thought I was average, at best."

"So sincere," she whispered, loving the feel of his hot breath and butterfly kisses on her skin. "You're more than average in every way."

"So are you," he whispered, his hands going to the back of the couch to encase her between his muscular arms. "And that nice dress is hugging you in all the right places."

"You think?" she asked innocently, shrugging so that the neckline plunged even deeper, revealing the curves of her breasts. "I thought it was a bit too much."

"I wasn't expecting it," he admitted, his soft chuckle against the exposed flesh of her shoulder making her shiver. "But I appreciate it more than you can possibly know."

"You don't seem too introverted right now," Lora commented, feeling his lips graze her shoulder. "I was worried you might be too shy to make the trip but I'm so glad you did."

Lora moved slowly to the bathroom leaving him an expectant smile. Hot water just expanded the new feelings at Lora's wet skin. His fingers touched slowly her back.

"I think we've waited long enough to meet," he reasoned, looking into her eyes now. "I've gotten to know you and you've somehow managed to bring me out of my shell. I cannot explain how happy that has made me."

"It was all you," she blushed, looking down at her feet. "It wasn't anything I did. I just encouraged you is all."

He tilted her chin upward now, his fingers cupping her jaw as his thumb traced aimlessly over her parted hot lips. "It was more than enough," he whispered, his lips almost touching hers now. "Is this alright? Is this what you want?"

"More than anything," she replied, entranced by the lustful look in his eyes. "I want you."

He didn't need to be told twice, his hands going to her backside to lift her smoothly off her feet and against him. She wrapped her legs around his hips now, as their bodies melded together as one. Their lips, battling one another for supremacy, were meeting in heated contact as they slowly began feeling one another out. They were breathlessly intertwined in one another's arms, unwilling to part even for a second as their hands roamed the other's body, as they stood under the steaming pour of the shower.

Hands brushing through her blond hair with a sigh of content, eyes closed as she rinsed the suds from her locks. Yet as she combed her fingers through his hair, her body jumped, eyes snapping open at the sound of the loud bang just outside her bathroom door.

That certainly hadn't been from next door, she would have been able to identify the sound being muffled through the wall. Leaving Jack behind, hands lifting to brush the droplets of water from her eyes, she hesitantly reached up and pulled her shower curtains open. Her bathroom, filled with steam, was empty; the sound seemed to have originated from her living space.

It was the distinct sound of her front door slamming closed, even over the sound of the shower pouring, she wouldn't mistake the sound of her own door. It was a noise that she had heard often, perhaps it was her best friend, Jenny, who had come home to drop something off out of the blue.

"Jenny? Is that you?" she called out, voice echoing off of the bathroom tiles coating the walls. Reaching out and wrapping her fingers around the slippery metal knob of the light.

She hoped to perhaps hear the young woman reply. In the silence, however, the only sound was the quiet dripping of the shower head. Faintly, in the absence of noise, she could hear the quiet sound of shuffling within her bedroom.

"Jenny?" she repeated quietly.

Brows furrowing in confusion, she reached up, wringing the moisture out of her hair before stepping out of the shower stall. Reaching out, she grabbed her towel, wrapping it around her body, tucking the knot at the top into itself to keep it suspended around her body. Grabbing the hair towel, she bent over and hurriedly twisted her hair up and out of the way.

Slowly making her way over to the door, the young woman reached out, only to pause. Drips of water seemed to be pouring down the from the frame of the door. She had taken longer, hotter showers than this but never did the condensation build this much.

Hesitantly, she pushed the door open, eyes glued to the floor where a puddle was slowly beginning to build. Her eyes only widened as her eyes flittered over to the floor of her room, there appeared to be wet footprints leading up to the bathroom door.

It wasn't raining outside, so surely no one would have been able to come in with wet feet and leave the marks. They didn't appear to be shoe prints either, the distinct shape of a bare foot, around the same size as her own.

Hesitantly, the young woman stepped into her bedroom, closing her bathroom door behind her, realized Jack is not there. As Lora slowly rose her head to inspect the rest of her apartment, her chest slowly filled with dread. The young woman gulped audibly, a horrified shudder running down her spine. She whispered "Jack?"

Although she knew that she had stepped out into her room, the sight before her was one that she didn't recognize. Seeming pouring out of the ceiling were streams of leaking, murky water. The light streaming through the windows seemed to have been blocked out completely. The walls, what had once been a simple white paint, was slowly distorting, right before her eyes, shifting, separating and darkening.

Before she knew it, her spotless pasty white walls had changed completely. Now before her were the decaying, moss covered planks almost like the inside of a ship.

Clutching her towel tighter to her chest, she panted shakily, staring down at her feet in horror, watching as dark black water slowly began to inch higher up her calves.

Eyes wide and logic fleeting, she hurriedly rushed towards the door, or rather she tried to with the water building around her shins, wading through the water as quickly as she could. The room echoed with the sound of the wooden boards around her creaking, and moaning much like a dilapidated old ship might.

The sound of the water trickling off the walls and the sound of her feet sloshing through the opaque water beneath her. As she slowly fought her way through the water, approaching the door, an unpleasant tingling feeling brushing against the nape of her neck.

Gasping sharply, she hurriedly turned in the water, frightened eyes widened as she checked the air around her.

A panicked gasp trapped itself in her compressing throat, her eyes widened in horror at the sight before her.

In what she thought had been her empty room, standing opposing her, was a woman. Her skin was a sickly pale shade, body clear of all clothing. Droplets of water trailed down her body, dripping down her bony wrists, off her fingertips and into the pool of water slowly building.

Her hair, as dark as night was soaked with water, framing her pale face. Eyes peered out at her through the dark curtains of her hair, what had once been eyes filled with life and colour had been dulled down with the cloudiness that came along with death.

Lora's blood felt like ice scratching at her veins with each terrified thump her heart gave. A part of her didn't want to take her eyes off of the ghost before her out of fear, another part of her wanted to turn tail and run.

The woman, gaze unrelenting, said nothing, she simply stood there and stared. Her gaze was chilling, freezing Lora's heart to the core.

"H-elp me--"

The young woman choked down a horrified scream, slapping a hand over her own mouth to choke down any sounds she might have made. Hesitantly, her stiff pupils turned towards the source of the voice, the search lead her to land her gaze upon her bed.

Lora whimpered, stomach turning in her abdomen as she stared in horror, laying out on her bed, wrinkled hand stretched out towards her was a corpse. The corpse of a man, his eyes wide and sunken into his head, he too seemed terrified of the woman standing in the corner. There wasn't a doubt in Lora's mind that she had done this to him.

"P-please-- help"

Her hazy eyes were steadily filling with horrified tears, as she stumbled back towards the door, she finally took notice of just how high the water had filled the room. The levels now reached her knees, knowing that she had to get out of it, knowing that perhaps when she opened the door the horror playing out before her might end, she hurriedly turned her back to the two mysterious figures.

Grabbing the soaked doorknob, she turned the handle and without so much as a second glance, rushed forward.

She had expected dry ground, she expected to see the bright lights and the dull walls of the hallway, she expected to turn around and see her empty room and for everything to go back to normal.

But that wasn't the case at all.

As she opened her bedroom door and leaped out into what was meant to be the empty hallway, she was met with nothing but cold and dark. Her feet had run out of ground, instead she was floating, floating in ice-cold water.

Lora couldn't see so much as a foot in front of her, the water that encased her was pitch black, murky and suffocating. Having barely had the chance to take a breath before she had thrown herself out of her room, her lungs were already beginning to burn for the need to inhale.

She didn't have the time to stop and think about her situation or the chance of a possible way out, her first instinct was to try and survive. Legs kicking through the water, her arms attempting to push herself up into what she could only assume to be the surface. The young woman didn't know which way was up, she could only swim and hope she was going in the right direction.

Lora didn't quite know how long she had been swimming for, she was in excruciating pain at this point. Her lungs screaming for air, head pounding from the pressure of the water, no doubt she had spent all this time swimming deeper.

Her muscles ached from how long and how hard she had been swimming. Eventually, her limbs had gone limp at her sides. Lora's arms simply floating above her head from the buoyancy of the water, bubbles pouring from her mouth faster than she could stop them.

She tried her best to move her fatigued arms, to cover her mouth to block the excess air from leaving her. She wanted to cry out, to scream for help, for someone, anyone to come and save her. But who would hear? Who would take any notice of her voice crying out from the deep?

Though her vision was hazy, mind spinning from the lack of oxygen, in the distance she could vaguely make out the sight of movement. Whatever it was, appeared to be a pure black cloud, wafting through the water, slowly approaching her. With each slow blink of her tired eyes, the cloud grew ever closer.

Although it was frightening, although she wanted to get as far away from that strange cloud as she could, she had no strength any longer. Her body had fallen limp, the hands that she had tried so hard to keep against her lips had begun floating away from her body once again.

The bubbles continued to leave her lips, floating towards the surface that was so far out of reach. Lora could feel the pressure growing stronger the deeper she succumbed into the deep. Though she was unable to control her limbs, her eyes remained pasted o-pen.

She could only float and watch in horror as the black cloud quickly picked up the pace, approaching at a much faster rate than it had been before, seemingly taking advantage of her paralyzed state.

It sped at her, charging like it was ready to devour her only to stop dead, coming to a sudden stop just before her nose.

She stared at the dark cloud, eyes glued open as she watched, awaiting her fate, simply staring and waiting for whatever it was going to do to her to happen.

It happened in the blink of an eye, a brief flash of light before out of the darkness of the cloud a face appeared.

The face of the woman who had been standing in her room, her cheeks were hollow, skin grey and discolored. The area around her eyes a dark black, blood vessels straining in the young woman's eyes, the white of her sclera tainted red.

More bubbles forced their way out of Lora's mouth as the fear in her heart amplified, she simply watched in horror as the woman before her took notice of her crippling fear. Slowly, a smile spread across her face, and beneath those pale blue lips, were teeth sharp and pointed.

Slowly breaching through the cloud, were the young woman's fingers, bony and pointed with sharp claws towards the tip. Her fingers were connected, webbed with membrane much like a fish's tail might have been.

The woman's hand clamped down on her shoulder, fingers pressing and bruising at her skin. With panic in her eyes, Lora's attempts to flee were fruitless and slowly, she was pulled into the depths. She was dragged down into what appeared to be a hole carved into the stone as she disappeared into the darkness.

"Hey, you okay?" Lora's thoughts were suddenly interrupted and she turned to look at Jenny sitting beside her. "Don't be nervous, It's only the recording. We have a great song."

"Are you ready?" The producer asked, before taking his seat. Lora walked into the booth and placed the headphones over her ears. Lora's voice was in the best shape. She was sure that she was completely ready to record their new song. Now, the only problem was her mind, she was in a panic thinking back on her last horror vision. Where is Jack? She has to perform, everybody is waiting for her. She was confident all this time, but the moment she put on the earphones, her heart started beating so fast, that Lora thought that she was going to faint. The staff was ready, Jenny had her guitar in hands, everyone was looking at Lora. It was so silent that Lora could hear her own heartbeat. After a second she showed a thumb as a symbol that she was ready to sing.

She shut her eyes and began to sing after the beat started. With every second, she immersed deeper in the rhythm. Lora tried to pour all the emotions into her singing, but everything goes wrong. She started singing again and again. She felt that she was losing part of her soul, her voice was disappearing, tears were coming into her eyes. Lora was trying hard but the things which were always easy for her now seemed the hardest.

The studio staff is baffled, something goes wrong again. They started talking in confusion.

Nik, the producer, stopped the session "It's the third time at the same place, you don't match your refrain, so we can do nothing, it's your money, I would sing it for you guys – but it's your turn, try it again."

"It's perfect time bee, we will get it." Jenny was trying to cheer up Lora. She was smiling over to her producer behind the glass, but Jenny still seemed confused and stressed.

Lora started to cry, looking down to the words on the page "Sorry babe, I'm out."

Jenny came close to Lora, starting to show wet eyes too. Lora thankfully smiled, looking up and hugging her friend. "Yes, baby we will fight together for our dream."

Lora asked with a curious face "But it's a lot of money, Jenny?

Money hasn't always been a problem for young rockstars, it especially wasn't a problem for Jenny, she did have rich parents, but she did not want to call them for money. Jenny told her parents that she could be responsible for herself, she was now adult, but she learned fast, that money is not something that can be earned easily.

Jenny shrugs her shoulders and said with a satisfied face "Don't care, my mom wanted to stop my dad, so you know my dad, he does care about art, then money."

Lora honestly said, "I love your dad, come on we'll give it one try more."

Lora took the headphones, starting rehearsal the same words full motivated again. She started to sing more passionately than ever. Lora was sure that this record was going to be the beginning of a big step for the band.

Lora showed a thumb to the studio staff as the symbol that she was ready, but her thumb was shaking from the stress and fear.

Lights off in the rec room, after the music started again. Lora closed her eyes starting to sing the first notes perfectly. Just when she thought that this time her voice was pure, she opens her eyes and sees the producer's room behind the glass filled with water. The corpse of studio staff inside, something moved mirroring in the glass and coming closer to Lora. She only saw a silhouette. Lora saw the ghost coming closer and closer, in a second Lora could be able to see the face and real shape of the ghost. Lora screams in fear and stops singing.

Jenny stopped, emotionally on the edge, she leaves the room. The recording is over. Lora follows Jenny very angrily making hard break, just leaving the studio crew waiting,

Studio staff baffled. Nik said soundlessly behind the glass "What the f..."

Lora, in her shock, took a break, now drinking a beer. Alcohol is the only thing which shreds Lora's messed up feelings and thoughts away. Now she knew, the evil ghost was always with her. Even though Lora could not always see them, she was always able to feel them.

Lora washed her face, trying to calm herself. Jenny didn't smile anymore, but still having faith in Lora. "Sorry, we just fucked up our session."

"Please Jenny, just one fucking time listen to me," Lora plea-ded. "I want to know what's going on with me? Tell me, how did you drop me out, why did you not find Jack?, tell me second for second, what's happened, I want just to know if I am full mad pack or if it's really the syndrome and postshock problems? Help me." Lora sounded scared.

Jenny was listening to Lora. Lora was begging her to tell the truth, but the only thing Jenny could do, was close her eyes and answer calmly, "You know I promised never to talk, its past, let it go, it was not my fault, it's not your fault, it just happened, if we talk more about it you will get worse, please stop, lets just work for some time, we have to."

Jimmy came closer to the girls, who were emotionally talking to each other. He puts his arm on Jenny's shoulder, comforting her, speaking to the girls "First record is not that easy I know, you have a half an hour left. Just relax five minutes and you will get it."

Lora made a break, leaving the room angrily. Still confused, they don't really know what is going on in Lora's mind and they don't know about the tragedy which just happened to Lora.

Jenny said, "F..." following Lora.

Jimmy informed, "You will never get this chance again guys"

"Piss off man, I'm losing my sister, she goes crazy, because of you," Jenny answered, leaving the room.

Jimmy looked at her in confusion, trying to figure out exactly, which part of the drama was his fault. Then he just laughed it away, because one of the staff guys were making fun of him.

Jimmy said to the studio staff "Sorry, they just left"

Nick turned on the chair, joking to Jimmy "It's obviously your fault Jimmy."

Then the guys went back to the recording room and continued talking about two beautiful weird girls, who just blew off their chance to have a great record session for their hit song.

The curse of a siren

Jack and Lora had spent a full day and night like that, wrapped up in one another, both were completely worn out. Lora felt wonton as if she had given in to a primal side of herself that she never again wanted to hide. Jack had thoroughly enjoyed this more spontaneous and dominant side of her and had made sure to allow her to take the lead whenever she wanted. Of course, their first night of bliss ended when early on the next day, while they were resting in one another's arms, Jenny came home.

"Knock, knock!" she called out, opening the front door. "Are you decent?"

Jack just smirked as Lora scrambled to her feet, pulling on the pair of shorts Jack had pulled off her only an hour before. She straightened her shirt and tried to tame her unruly hair as she emerged from her room, a smile on her face.

"That's what I like to see," Jenny chuckled, winking at her friend. "How have you been? I hadn't heard from you since I left, so I thought I'd come and check up on you two."

"I am in trouble," Lora smiled, nodding at the bedroom. "Haven't left the apartment."

"I see that," her roommate smirked, walking to the living room window and opening the blinds. "Look at what a beautiful day it is. Let's open the windows and air this place out."

"Something bad happened!" Lora exclaimed.

She sat next to her best friend on her own bed, pillow hugged to her chest as she retold the events that had passed. Fear was plastered on her face, it was clear that the vision she had, had been something quite traumatizing for her.

Jenny bit her lip, reaching out to place a gentle hand upon her trembling friend's shoulder.

"I'm sure it was nothing Lora" she mumbled gently.

"Maybe it was just the build-up of stress from school, y'know? A really bad dream, I've had really bad dreams because of stress too!" she assured.

Lora bit her lip, peering up at her beloved friend nervously. She sighed deeply and ran her hands down her face before nodding in agreement.

"You're probably right, I've had nightmares before, I'm probably just thinking into it too much"

Jenny smiled warmly in agreement, and as she moved her hand off of the young woman's shoulder, she watched as her sleeve dropped off. Jenny recoiled with a gasp, pulling her hand back hurriedly.

Lora tensed to hear her friend react in such a way, trying her best to glance down at her own shoulder to check what caused the woman's distress. As she glanced down at her own shoulder, she could see it clear as day, a hand-shaped bruise covered her pale skin.

"Before you do anything else, you should go to Ursula to get that checked out" Jenny mumbled, worry laced in her voice.

Towards the black and blue fingertips of the bruise on her shoulder, there were long scratches where the siren's nails had dragged across her fragile skin.

Biting her lip she reached up to place a hesitant hand over the wound, just looking at it made her reminisce on the horrible memories from the illusions she had witnessed.

Glancing down at her lap, the Lora took a deep breath before glancing up and meeting her friend's eyes.

"In my visions, whenever it drags me down into that hole, I end up dying" she breathed out. Pulling her sleeve up her shoulder to hide the bruise out of self-consciousness.

"I want the illusions to end-- I'm gonna try and research it, maybe-- maybe that'll give me some answers? Maybe that'll help it all stop?"

Jenny glanced up at her friend nervously, she took a deep breath before she dipped her head with a smile of reassurance.

"I'll help you."

They spent hours researching, looking into anything that sounded remotely like the display that Lora would see in her visions.

Eventually, Lora happened upon it, the article depicting the hole that she knew all too well. Along with the description of the location, the article came with the tale. The old myth of the Loreley siren and her sorrowful past. Reading over the events, Lora's heart ached for Loreley.

As she read over the site, it was clear that her visions weren't visions at all. It was all real, every last detail that she had recalled, right down to the hole she had been dragged through and died in. The hole itself was real, and in fact, many people had lost their lives there.

Lora opened an online comment; " The ghost of the siren cast out to the river all those years ago is still there, she would always be there, but people these days don't believe in ghosts."

Lora's brows furrowed and she bit her lip, leaning back in her seat with a quiet sigh as she tore her gaze away from her laptop screen. She wanted this curse to be over, she didn't want to have to deal with this fear for the rest of her life.

According to the article, the site of her horror had been turned into a tourist attraction. Raising her hand to chew on the nail of her thumb out of nervousness, she needed all of this to end, she needed to go back to living her ordinary life.

Taking a deep breath she furrowed her brows and nodded towards herself.

With her mind made up, Lora decided that she would travel out to the tourist attraction, in hope to get answers.

Lora just blushed, nodding as her roommate cracked the window in the living room and the kitchen before going to her own room to open the window. She waved lazily at Jack as she passed by Lora's room where he was pulling on his t-shirt.

"No classes today?" Jenny asked, leaning against the counter now.

"I decided I can miss a couple," Lora smirked, moving to the kitchen to make some coffee. "We're thinking of going on a tour of the original Lureberg along the river. Want to come?"

"Absolutely," Jenny chuckled, grabbing the coffee out of the cupboard for Lora while she fills the coffee pot. "I think a couple of hours of relaxation will do us all some good."

"What kind of plans are you two hatching?" Jack asked, sitting in the stool on the opposite side of the counter.

"The Rhein tour," Lora smiled, scooping out some coffee. "We'll have some fast food and then we'll see if they still have tickets. Sound good?"

"Very," Jack nodded, glancing out the window. "I'm starving."

"I bet," Jenny winked, nudging Lora before heading to her room.

"What do you want to eat?" Lora asked, starting the coffee pot now. "I can cook something if you'd like…"

"Whatever you'd like," Jack smiled, reaching across the counter and taking her hand. "I'm so glad we can do it together."

"So am I," she admitted, lacing their fingers together. She then walked around the end of the counter and wrapped her arms around his torso, holding him close. He smelled of pine and musk and she inhaled deeply, enjoying the warmth of his arms as they wrapped around her.

The morning was full of laughter and food, Lora offering to make a good breakfast for all three of them. It was a large breakfast and when they were finally done, Lora felt like she wouldn't be able to move, let alone hike through the Loreley tour. However, she showered, dressed, and waited for Jack to get ready as Jenny spoke to her boyfriend Henry, on the phone.

Once Jack was ready, Jenny offered to drive, telling Henry she'd call him later before following both of them downstairs to the lobby. That was the nice thing about their apartment complex – it was close to campus but far enough downtown to warrant a lobby.

The ride to the museum and trail down by the river coast was longer than usual, traffic on a Monday morning more hectic than Lora would have known. She was always in class or working at this time, so it was a new experience she enjoyed in their small university city. After patrolling the parking lot, they finally found a space, parking the car and making their way toward the pier and museum. It was a large modern building, set on the city's largest pier on the bay.

"Tickets are still available," the vendor said, sitting in her small box behind the thick glass window. "How many would you like and for which package?"

"What are the options?" Jenny asked, looking up at the pricing screen.

"We have just the museum, where you can explore the city's maritime history and the ship displays out on the docks," she explained, pointing to the first bracket. "Then there is the museum and boat tour out on the bay. The last one is the museum, boat tour, and a tour of the Loreley caves and their geological formations. You can also do individual options such as just the boat tour or just the caves."

"Let's just do them all!" Jenny smirked, looking back at Lora and Jack. "My treat?"

"You sure?" Lora asked, glancing up at Jack and then back to Jenny. "We can just do the caves."

"If we're playing hooky, we might as well do it right," Jenny nodded, turning back to the vendor. "Three tickets for all three options."

Lora had to admit that she was glad that Jenny offered to pay. She was running low on money, having bought out food the past few nights. The museum, which Lora had not had the time or interest in before, was pleasantly simple. It had ship recreations, sunken skeletons of ships from eras long past, and there were even displays of treasures and archaeological findings. What was more refreshing, and interesting, was the pier beyond the museum where two rebuilt boats from the nineteenth century sat bobbing in the foam.

"They're smaller than I thought," Jack admitted, looking over the larger, old wooden ship. "Look, we can board it."

Lora giggled at how excited he was, noticing the twinkle in his eye as he gently pulled on her hand. She nodded, following him as Jenny admired one of the huge ropes used to attach it to the dock. The ship was bobbing gently as they explored, walking across the deck and underneath to see the storage and sleeping quarters as well as where the cannons were housed. When they came back up, they took the stairwell to the captain's quarters.

"Would you look at that," Jack laughed, pointing at the huge bed that was bolted to the floorboards. "Lucky guy got a plush feather bed while the rest of the crew sleeps in hammocks."

"It does look comfortable," Lora smirked, walking over to it. She stepped over the low velvet rope and sank down, feeling the mattress give way beneath her. She almost sunk into it, lowering with a giggle onto the plush bedding.

"Naughty," Jack replied, glancing around quickly before joining her on the bed. He hovered over her, laying on his side with a grin. She admired his green eyes now, watching him as he looked her over with a hungry gaze.

"What are you thinking?" she asked with a smirk, brushing some of his hair out of his face.

"I'm thinking I want to take you on a boat," he replied, trailing his finger down her cheek. "Somewhere beautiful, warm, and sunny. We can just relax, have our own bed anchored to the floor…"

"Who's naughty now?" she asked, snuggling up against him.

"We better not," he groaned, wrapping an arm around her waist. "We'll get caught."

"You're right," she sighed, kissing his shoulder gently before wiggling to get out of the bed.

"There you two are," Jenny said, coming into the cabin. "I've been looking everywhere for you. The boat tour begins in ten minutes."

"Let's go!" Jack nodded, standing up off the bed and grabbing Lora's hand. The trio hurried to the docks, making it to the ship just before they were about to close the gate. It was a modern boat with a flat bottom with some other tourists on it.

"This is going to be great," Jack nodded, finding them some seats near the railing overlooking the Rhein landscape and castles from middle age.

The beautiful movement of the leaves, dancing in the wind on both mountains as the ship slowly cruised causing ripples on the Rhein river. Lora inhaled and released the air, folding her arms over her chest as she stared ahead at the wonderful scenery.

"Fill thee." She felt arms circle around her waist and a light kiss on her neck, a chuckle escaped her lips leaving behind a smile. She turned her head to his side, seeing his blond hair and white t-shirt swaying in the wind and face glowing under the orange sunlight.

"Fill thee too." She replied with a smile, watching him place his arms over the railing still looking into her eyes with his green ones.

"You seem happy this morning, Hope I had a hand in it." Lora chuckled, lightly hitting his shoulder. Jake smiled.

They stood aboard the deck of the tourist liner, glancing to one another. The ship would take them to the tourist attraction, but it was up to Lora and Jenny to seek out the cave themselves.

"Isn't she beautiful?" Lora asked staring straight ahead.

"Yes, she is," Jake said looking at her legs.

"I'm talking about the statue." Lora chuckled, noticing he was still staring at her. Jake turned his attention to the long rock on the river, with a statue of a naked woman sitting at the edge.

"She lured sailors with her voice and beauty, causing their heads to hit the rock and sink along, just like me." Jake said still staring at Lora.

"I can relate." Lora turned to Jake in confusion. "But I don't make people fall into a river...I only love to sing." Jake turned to look at the statue, a fond smile on his face.

"Time to go, we want to see the original." Lora and Jake both turned, seeing Jenny in her usual black shorts and shirt, this time in white sneakers; approach them with one bag pack behind her and two in both hands. The breeze was quite cool, the fresh spray making Lora's skin feel tight as they cruised out into the Loreley dock.

As it pulled up to the dock, the tourists filed off of the boat, amongst them, Jack, Jenny, and Lora followed. They used the distraction of the tour guides instructions to slip away from the group, sneaking out of the crowd. Making sure that no one was following, they rushed away.

The chirping of birds and breaking of twigs underneath their feet was all Lora could hear as they walked deeper into the rock formation, the tourist attraction with Loreley rock still in view.

With the page of the article pulled up on her phone, Lora guided her friend to the scene of her nightmares, following the guide left in the article.

Glancing down at her phone with furrowed brows to make sure that she was following the right directions, as she lifted her head to check where she was going, the young woman gasped sharply and paused in her step.

"Lora?" Jenny mumbled in confusion as she stepped up behind her friend.

"This is it" she breathed out in response.

Jenny blinked in shock, hurriedly stepping up to Lora's side to get a look for herself, checking the area the young woman was staring at.

"Whoa, come look at this." Jake went around Lora, staring at the sight before them. They moved to the valley of the old Rhine, looking for original Loreley rock where many ships had sunk. Behind the trees the first metallic towers were visible. The ship cemetery with many old rusty wracks stood next to each other. The place was anything but a tourist attraction. It's hard to believe that the beautiful young Loreley was the cause of all the giants that crashed and sank into the Rhine.

After looking inside of an old tourist shipwreck they moved to another sunken ship, a trading vessel from the eighteenth century. The wooden frame was rotted but you could make out the shape and the crucial parts of the small merchant ship. The history was fascinating, but the next sunken ship was the most beautiful. It had sunk and become entangled in a large formation of rocks, the surface so was perfectly visible. It was a seventeenth-century galley, with a huge mast and intricate wooden features that had eroded to just a frame and a few stray rotted pieces of wood.

They stopped and let the scenery take effect on them. Behind the wracks a dark cave, with huge rocks and a pile of dead leaves at the mouth.

It looked ghostly and for a moment, in the whipping of wind and the hissing of echoes, Lora thought she could hear a voice. It was quiet but it grew louder with the wind, the river spray feeling almost cold, burning her cheek as the horrific noise became louder. She then spotted it, behind a rock formation, behind the ghostly vessels, was a small waterfall. She gasped aloud making Jenny and Jack look at her curiously.

"What is it?" Jenny asked, following her gaze. "What?"

"Are you okay?" Jack asked, wrapping his arm around her tightly.

"Just Déjà vu," Lora said, tearing her eyes away from the horrible sound that was set in her ears.

"I'd recognize that rock anywhere, the opening of the cave has to be there," she breathed out shakily. Fingers trembling as she balled her hands into fists at her sides and shoved her phone back into her pocket, hurriedly climbing down off of the pier towards the cave.

Jenny reached out for her friend hesitantly, the cave beneath the pier didn't look safe at all, especially with all the horrible visions that Lora had including the cave.

"Odd," Jenny said, looking about. "It's the original Loreley hill?"

"No," Lora admitted, moving closer to Jack.

"You're shaking," he said softly, watching her.

"I'm just cold," she assured, looking back over her shoulder at the way back. It was a calm, bright afternoon but it was also brisk. They got closer to the rock formation. First rain drops fell down, some seconds later it started to rain. By the time they had gotten back to the old wreck, their clothes were all damp as were their shoes and hair.

"Should we skip the Loreley cave?" Jenny asked, looking at how pale Lora had become.

"We probably should," Jack nodded, his arm still around Lora to support her.

"No," Lora said, shaking her head. "I need to know what she wants or if am really mad."

"You need a hot bath," Jenny nodded, watching her friend wearily.

"Let's just look inside," Jake insisted, not wanting to ruin Lora's hope to get answers. "It's only a half-hour…"

"Fine, but if you start feeling sick, we're leaving," Jenny warned, turning toward the entrance.

Lora had started to gain her wits again as they approached the cave entrance.

Lora kept pace, looking about her at the cave formations. The noise the wind made inside the cave was amazing and she couldn't help but appreciate it. She also enjoyed the echo of their voices as they descended onto a steel causeway overlooking a deep grotto. They discovered the geological formations and different minerals that could be found there.

"This is what we wanted to see. A wet, dark cave." Jake said, still staring at the cave.

"You're not the only one," Lora said, following Jake into the cave with an enthusiastic Jenny behind her. Jake picked up a flashlight from his backpack and turned it on, revealing the same color rocks forming the insides of the cave. They walked deeper into the cave until the mouth could no longer be seen.

"Wait," Jake said, stopping them in their tracks. "Do you hear that?" He asked, paying close attention to the sound.

"Yes…water," Lora said, and they quickened their pace after noticing light in the distance, the sound getting louder. Taking a deep breath through her clenched jaws, she built her confidence and slowly descended, following her friend down towards the light source.

"Wow," Lora said, once they reached the source.

A clear pond with huge rocks on the side against the walls of the cave. A huge hole in the roof, with water gently pouring out if it like a waterfall, accompanied by a stream of light, giving the pond a blue glow and lighting up the cave beautifully.

"I have to take a pic, here is beautiful," Jenny said, making her way to the rocks. They carefully walked on each rock, holding the wall for support. "They look more beautiful up-close." She jumped from the final rock onto the bank before walking hastily to them.

Lora got down from the rock, with help from Jake. She walked up to the big round stone, standing beside Jenny admiring them

"Someone has been here recently." Lora turned her attention to Jake squatting in front of the wall studying something on the rock. She hastily walked up to him and bent down, taking a peek.

"A writing." She said, looking at the wet stone site.

"Jenny, come and translate this…It's german." She said, still studying the words. They looked like they were just written in stone.

" Ich weiß nicht, was soll es bedeuten, die Luft ist kühl und es dunkelt, die schönste Jungfrau sitzet, den Schiffer im kleinen Schiffe, Ich glaube, die Wellen verschlingen...its the song about Loreley." Jenny heard Lora sing the words in a small voice beside her. Before she finished the words, they heard a thunder crackle outside. Jenny straightened her body. The thunder echoed deep into the cave followed by a whispering sound that came out of the darkness of the cave.

"What did you say?" Jenny asked, still starring at Lora.

"What?" Lora turned her head to see Jenny, looking at her expectantly.

"What do you mean?" Jenny replied in confusion.

"You mentioned my name." Lora chuckled and rolled her eyes focusing her attention back on the way back.

"No, I didn't," Jenny said in confusion, before turning her attention back to Lora.

"Jenny, It's not funny." She turned her attention back to Jack, seeing him spotting the light into the darkness of cave.

"I hear it too, I mean Its just the rain, I will check it." Jack said, moving into the dark.

The whispering noise became louder and came out of the darkness towards them.

"Seriously, I didn't mention…" Lora caught a glimpse of something moving toward them out of the dark bottom. "Guys, its water" She said, still staring at the pond. Jake got up from his squatting position and walked up to the pond, looking inside.

"We move back," Jake said, turning to look at Lora. "I think it's time to go." He said, noticing her discomfort. Jenny took a picture of the three, quickly unplugging one before following them.

Lora bit her lip and glanced around nervously, she wasn't quite sure what she had been looking for. Perhaps answers? But there was nothing to be seen here, nothing but rotting ships and bellowing wind. Biting her lip she took a deep breath before slowly nodding.

"Yeah, let's get out of here"

As the girls slowly turned, Jack followed to walk back the way they came, the sound of the howling wind and crashing water hit the place. Lora gasped sharply, a familiar feeling tickling at the base of her ankles. Her head shot down to peer down at her legs, begging that it was just her imagination, that her horrid visions weren't coming to light.

Lora looked down at the water, which seemed to be getting closer by the second as they walked on the cave. She raised her head to look at the water pouring from the hole, increase in quantity and pace.

"What?" Lora said after Jake stopped moving. She was about to say another word but stopped. The rushing sound of water getting louder from the tunnel.

"What the hell." She heard Jake cuss and shifted her gaze to see a huge wave of water gush from the tunnel pouring into the cave.

"Hold the light in front," Lora shouted over the noise of the water gushing. She looked down feeling something wet on her feet and noticed how much the water had risen, almost covering the rocks. They went on, the water had risen very quickly to their knees. Soon all three were wet up to the valley. With great relief they saw the daylight, it was the entrance to the cave. A scream emanated from behind Lora and she turned to see Jenny clutching onto the rock, her lower body buried in the water and her backpack floating on top.

Jenny's fearful shriek was telltale enough that this was very real, around her legs was a pool of murky water, too dark to even see her own feet.

The water was building fast as they stood at the opening of the cave, climbing up the length of their legs. Jenny was gripping onto her arms tightly, eyes wide in panic as she stared down at the rapidly building water.

Lora looked to the opening of the cave that they had wandered through, there was no way to safely hop over the rocks to hurriedly step out. She took a shaky, fearful breath and took her friend's hand tightly, she would have to take initiative, show Jenny that it wasn't as scary as it seemed.

The young woman winced as she dropped down into the water, careful not to slip, the water already reached her chest. She squeezed her eyes closed and willed away the horrid memories clouding her mind. Panting shakily, she bunched her shoulders up to her ears and held out her hands for Jenny.

"Jenny!" Lora shouted carefully walking over the rock with Jake close behind her. She held one hand and Jake held the other, trying to pull her body out.

"Move, we're gonna have to walk our way out before it fills up too far," Jack said pulling about the water the backpacks of them.

Jenny looked apprehensive, a look of horrified disdain on her face, but Jenny wasn't stupid, she knew that it was the only opportunity they might have to finally escape and get back.

Gripping onto Lora's hands for support, Jenny carefully hopped off of the boulder she had been standing upon, shivering as soon as her upper body dipped into the water. Teeth chattering, she nodded to her braver friend so they could continue their journey back.

Slowly, as the three waded through the steadily rising water, they came to a sudden stop.

"D-Did you hear that?" Jenny choked out nervously.

Lora took a shaky breath, she did, it was unlike the sounds of the rushing water, nor like the sounds of their own bodies sloshing through the waves. There was a third person amongst them, even as they stopped, they could hear the sound of the body slowly wading through the water.

They turned hurriedly, facing the source of the sound in hopes of catching it out and perhaps put their worries to rest. There was nothing behind them, no sight of a body around them, nothing other than the sight of ripples in the water.

Gentle waves shaped in the form of an arrow, slowly pushing towards them, it wasn't hard to figure out what it was. There was something beneath the water, the way it swam causing the ripples atop the water, it was approaching them, and Lora could safely say that it wouldn't be friendly.

Slowly, the two girls and Jake began to back away, too horrified to dare think of facing whatever it was that might be approaching.

Appearing to notice that the young adults were stepping further and further away, the ripples grew larger, the sloshing sound growing louder. Whatever it was, it was fast approaching now.

They stumbled back, attempting to get as far away from the ripple as they possibly could. Hurriedly turning to face the mouth of the cave, the source of light and their possible sanctuary. They looked to be getting close, hope building in their chest. That hope was quickly extinguished.

"Something is there…"A force suddenly pulled Jenny down into the water swiftly, leaving behind light echoes of her scream. The sound of her panicked scream cut off by the gurgling of water was heartbreaking. Faster than Lora could turn her head, Jenny was dragged under.

"No, No Jenny! "Lora shouted, attempting to jump into the water which was now neck high, but Jake held her back in time. Lora gasped, lunging forward to try to grab Jenny but she had already gone in, the water splashing around them. Jack's eyes were wide as he watched, stepping forward to make sure Lora didn't fall in as well.

"Jenny? Jenny?!" Lora called out, screaming her friends name in horror, she should never have done this, she should never have put her friend's life at stake.

She hurriedly turned towards Jack, digging at the water as though it would surface her friend.

"She's not coming up," Lora cried out, moving around Jack mindlessly. "We have to help."

"Jenny!" she cried out, voice echoing back at her.

"Wait here." He said, handing his backpack over and jumping into the water before she could protest. Lora stared at the pond, clutching unto the bag, the water level rising.

"Lora…a" she heard the faint voice echo in the cave. She looked around her environment, heart pounding in her chest. She turned her gaze to the water moving slowly back. "Please Jack, don't let me alone." Something swam past her and touched her left leg. "Jack" she called, feeling her heartbeat in her head. The same horror starts paralyzing her. Her own voice screaming back at her was all she could hear, the ripples among the surface of the water had ceased.

She was all alone in the cave, or so she thought, just as her curiosity grew and her defenses lowered, a bruising grip that felt all too familiar snapped down around her ankle.

Eyes wide, the young woman gasped sharply, squeezing her eyes closed, and before she knew it, something suddenly grabbed her leg, pulling her swiftly into the water, denying her the chance to scream.

She looked up at the top seeing the light above the water as the force pulled her deeper. She tried to scream, stretching her hands upwards, but every effort produced bubbles. The cold water surrounded her like hundreds of sharp needles, prickling her skin. Her vision was getting blurry by the second and she looked down. However, before she could comprehend what she saw, Lora froze, eyes going wide. There, below her spinning and clouded in the dark water were a set of familiar black eyes. The panic overwhelmed her, making her kick frantically toward the surface but she found she couldn't move. She let out a scream, cold water rushing into her mouth and nose as she tried to look after Jack and Jenny. She was helpless. She refused to look down, crying out as cold water seemed to burn her nose, lungs, and eyes. She was about to give up, to let the creature in the darkness kill her when she felt the most horrifying sensation. A bigger snake tail, she thought before the world went dark.

The synchronizing movement of their lips as they hastily ripped each other's clothes, moaning with every single touch. Jake pushed her on the bed, making his way to unbuckle his belt, looking at her with lust in his eyes. Lora quickly removed her shorts, ripped shirt and bra, leaving her in her white lace panties with sweat streaking down her body. Jake dropped his pants, staring at her firm breast and hard pink nipples. He climbed the bed, taking one nipple into his mouth before sucking on it.

Lora's head fell back on the sofa, back arched and a loud moan escaped her lips. Her eyeballs rolled behind her socket. She placed her hands into his locks, gently kneading his skull.

"Beautiful," he whispered, trailing kisses across her collar bone before gently flicking his tongue out over the exposed swollen flesh. She could feel the blush rising in her cheeks and neck but didn't care, fully engulfed in the sensation of his lips on her flesh. He noticed the blush, pulling back and blowing cool air across her neck and chest making more goosebumps form there.

She didn't stop him as his hands went back down to her bottom, hoisting her firmly against his body as he looked up at her now. He was carrying her, her legs wrapped firmly around his hips as he sauntered to her bedroom. He kicked the door shut behind him with a snap, never taking his eyes off Lora's blushing face as he carried her to her bed. Once at the edge of the bed he slowly lowered her down, her soft curves pressing against him as she sat, legs still parted around his own as he stood above her. His eyes were full of admiration and wonderment as he took her in, her swollen lips and chest quivering under his gaze. She didn't want to admit that she loved the way he hungrily took her in, his hands going to the hem of his own shirt. He pulled it up over his head in one swift action, tossing it to the floor unceremoniously.

Lora admired his body at the moment, noting the curvature of his hips and the way it came down in a V-shape below the hem of his pants. She liked that his stomach was toned but not obnoxiously so. He had a little bit of a stomach, but it wasn't flabby, the dark trail of hair leading down from his chest to his navel and below set her imagination ablaze. He had some slight hairs across his wide chest as well, her hand reaching out to press against it as he watched her arch her back below him.

Without a word, he lowered himself to capture her lips again, grabbing her around her hips and hoisting her up so she was now lying in the middle of the bed. Her legs were still parted around him as he lowered himself down to her, his tongue exploring her mouth slowly as his hands traced the curve of her body. His fingers danced from her knee, up her thigh and hip, and alongside the curve of her stomach before stopping, painfully hovering over the swell of her chest still confined behind the tight red material.

She could feel herself arching against him as his lips trailed painfully slowly across her jawline and down her neck, stopping at her sternum as he hovered over her, hands pressed into the mattress on either side of her arms. She almost sighed in relief when his hands reached around behind her, unzipping the dress as his lips suckled at her neck. She moaned in approval as his lips trailed their way back down her neck toward the now loosened dress around her chest. She could hear him audibly groan as he pulled the dress down to reveal the red lacy material of her bra.

His hands then fumbled for a moment under her, pinching at the clasps of the red garment before finally releasing it. They both let out a heady sigh as her chest jiggled loose from the satin and lace material. She felt relieved, the anticipation of his flesh against hers the only thought in her head as the tingling sensation spread from her stomach up to her now partially exposed flesh. She could feel her flesh under the loose material harden as he pulled the material from her body, her arms slipping out of the straps of both her dress and bra to reveal the porcelain firmness and fullness of her chest. She blushed brightly as he took in the sight, his hips pressing more firmly to her core as the dress was rolled down to only cover her stomach now. She could feel his rough hands running slowly over her knees, thighs, and hips before stopping at her side, just below the swells of her breasts. He pulled away from her now to fully admire her body below him and she could feel the need in his gaze as he took in the rosy peaks of her round flesh, licking his lips hungrily. She could feel his hips rhythmically pressing against her as he stared down at her from above. He was kneeling between her legs, her thighs squeezing his hips tightly every time he pressed his firmness against her.

Their eyes were hungrily taking one another in, Lora's need to feel him touch her overwhelming every sense as she stared up at him. She wanted him more than she ever wanted anything, and it was a heady mixture of lust and a soulful bond that she couldn't quite explain, running deeper than any relationship she ever had. She needed him to possess her just as much as she needed to possess him. It was almost animalistic the way her body began to react to his, pressing more fervently against his hardened member as his hips unconsciously thrust against her.

Then, without warning his hand came up and squeezed her breast between his fingers. She let out a heated cry of ecstasy as the sensation exploded across her flesh, encouraging him to press on as his other hand massaged her other breast slowly. It was pure bliss, her rosy peaks instantly hardening as his fingers jiggled and squeezed her ample flesh. Her eyes closed as her back arched, a soft chuckle of satisfaction escaping his lips as she reacted to his touch.

"Feels good?" he asked, his breath hot against her flesh as he lowered his face to better appreciate the hardening bliss of her chest.

"Yes," she moaned, her hands going to grasp his forearms as his hands both closed around the underside of her breasts. He began jiggling them a little harder now, watching the blissful smile spread across her lips. She cried out in surprise and excitement when his lips closed around a hardened pink bud. He didn't stop, even as she wiggled beneath him, his lips closing around the peak and suckling roughly at her flesh. She felt the heat in her stomach and breast spread across her entire body, the lavish wetness of his mouth on her hardened nipple making her whimper aloud.

"Mmmhmm…" he moaned against her nipple, suckling at it harder as he pinched the other rosy peak between his finger and thumb. "You like this?" he asked, his hot breath fanning against her wet and sensitive nipple as he drew it into his mouth yet again.

"So much," she managed to whisper, the ecstasy her body was feeling incomparable to any other sensation she has ever felt. "Good," he breathed, running his tongue quickly and roughly over the swollen pink bud. She shivered, crying out as he continued to lick at her hungrily. It was then that she felt his hand sliding down from the breast his lips ware suckling to her hip.

"Relax," he instructed, feeling her starting to tense up as his hand grazed her navel before wandering lower. Her hips instinctively bucked underneath him as his hand slid beneath her lacy panties. Her eyes widening in disbelief as her body shook with pleasure. Her breathing was erratic. Her body was opening to all these new pleasures and she couldn't help but feel breathless at the way his hands and lips made her feel.

It didn't help that Jack was teasing her, blowing cool air against the already swollen and sensitive flesh. Then, as if something exploded within her, she felt his other hand press firmly, almost painfully, against her core. She let out a yelp, making Jack pause and watch her face as his fingers pulled her panties down over her hips and thighs, lifting one leg up to his shoulder so he could slip the thin garment from her flesh.

The ecstasy was incomparable, her hips bucking and thrusting at an alarming pace, like an erotic dance as she was brought to climax within a matter of minutes. When she had finally calmed back down, her breathing returning to normal, Jack kissed her lips, his body pressing against hers wantonly. She knew what he wanted and after everything he had made her feel, she knew she couldn't settle for anything less. She had to have all of him and the look that he saw in her eyes only confirmed his hopes.

"My swallow." He moaned looking into her eyes. Lora felt something new. She looked into his eyes and nodded. She clutched onto the sheets tightly, as pain coursed through her abdomen.

"Sorry." He apologized, sinking deeper into her while placing a kiss on her forehead. He began to move slowly, increasing his pace by the second with encouragement from her moans. Soon the only sound that could be heard in the stateroom was the slapping of skin and the sinful moans from Lora's lips.

Lora rolled her eyes behind her socket; she felt pleasure, immense pleasure, that it was almost painful. Her breath hitched…she couldn't breathe…everything was dark.

"Wake up!" the voice begged, frantically close to her ear. "Lora, please, wake up!"

She could feel the world around her becoming heavier, her own suspended body being forced down until it reached a solid surface, her eyes roaming the vast darkness about her. Then, she felt it, the pulse jolting her awake. She forced her eyes opened and began to cough, catching up with her breathing and looked around. The white walls were replaced by rock walls. She struggled to take in the scenery, her eyes burning from the light and the cold water that still ran down her face into her eyes and nose.

"It's ok, breathe." She heard a voice and looked up to see Jenny looking down at her with concern in her eyes, and then everything came back. She coughs up, quickly raised her head to the site, noticing they were still in the cave, in front of the tunnel, the massive rain still falling, rising water level high and everything was back to the way it was.

"She's alright," Jenny's voice came, a hand grasping at her arm. "Lora, can you hear me?"

"What..?" she asked, her voice hoarse and raw. "What happened?"

"You fell in," Jenny replied, her voice quiet as Lora finally realized they were back up on the cave entrance. She was lying on her back, looking at the stone ceiling of the cavern. Jenny was kneeling beside her as an EMT hovered over them both. The tour guide, another EMT, and a police officer were all standing a short distance away, conversing quietly. Lora didn't know what to make of it, trying to sit up.

She was stopped by a friendly hand, urging her to remain laying down until they could get a stretcher. She didn't feel any pain though, sure she could stand and regain her balance rather quickly. However, Jenny just looked at her worriedly, looking up at the EMT with a hopeless expression. Something was wrong and Lora wasn't sure what.

Then, as if a light switch had flicked on, she realized that Jack wasn't there. She looked around swiftly, making Jenny bite her lip worriedly as her friend realized her boyfriend was missing.

"Where is Jack?" She asked, looking around.

"I don't know?" She heard her say, and saw the sad expression on her face. "I sear…"

"Jack!" Lora shouted, interrupting her. She was losing her sight.

"Where is Jack, Jenny?" Lora was becoming impatient, her voice becoming a little louder with every word.

"Miss, you need to calm down or I will have them sedate you," the EMT informed, a firm hand grasping her upper arm.

"What about Jack?!" she asked, becoming impatiently furious.

"I know this is hard," the EMT interjected, trying to calm her. "And I am sorry but, we pulled you out of the water in an almost catatonic state. We were able to restart your heart but… there is no sign of your boyfriend."

"We will do all that we can to find him, miss. But for now, we need to get you out of this cave and to a hospital."

"Here is the stretcher," the EMT said, nodding at the two men carrying the plastic equipment down the rocks. "Please, let's get you out of here."

"He has to be here," Lora whispered, tears leaking from her eyes. Lora slowly blacks out "Please, you have to find him."

"We will do our best," the policeman said, placing a hand on her shoulder. "Come on, let's get you to the hospital."

She couldn't stop sobbing, couldn't stop shaking as the EMTs helped her onto the stretcher, covering her with thick blankets before strapping her in. She could feel Jenny's hand the whole time holding hers, squeezing gently as Lora cried. The warmth of her friend's hand and the soft whispers of reassurance were all she could comprehend, her body so weak and tired that soon, the sirens of the ambulance and echoes of voices soon faded into the distance.

Lora had called Jenny to her room, she needed to prove that what she was seeing wasn't fake, it wasn't all in her head like the doctor thought. Jenny, still traumatized from the events in the cave, was apprehensive at first; but at the look in her best friend's eyes, she simply couldn't refuse. So as Lora sat in her room, taking deep, shuddering breaths as she prepared herself for the next vision she knew was bound to come, she repeated the doctor's words in her head.

They sat together atop Lora's bed, clutching each other's hands tightly. Lora's eyes were closed, focusing on her deep, shuddering breaths heaving at her chest. From the way Jenny's hand tightened around her own suddenly, she knew that it had started, the familiar sound of the walls trickling with water reaching her ears.

Lora opened her eyes slowly, glancing around her room and watching as the water continued to steadily rise. With each passing day, the more vicious these attacks became, the water now flooding the room at a frightfully fast rate.

Jenny glanced between to the water and Lora's face, she seemed oddly calm, yet Jenny knew that the turmoil raging inside her best friend's head would definitely differ.

Slowly, Lora leaned towards the water, hand slowly outstretched towards the water surface. Jenny's eyes widened in horror, to see her friend leaning so close to the water, to see her daring to even touch it.

As Lora's hand slowly lowered towards the water, Jenny could only watch in horror as a pale grey hand reached out of the water below. Webbed fingers stretching open to slowly wrap around Lora's wrist, Jenny's free hand was still clutched tightly in Lora's.

She only had the time to squeeze her eyes closed before the two were both yanked into the water.

Lora awoke in the hospital, hooked to bags and tubes as Jenny sat in the chair next to the bed. When she tried to get up, she realized her movement was restricted. This woke Jenny and she quickly unstrapped her from the bed, taking her hand in her own. Lora listened in horror and grief as Jenny explained that after four hours of searching the grotto and the caves, the police had come up with nothing. They took rescue teams of dogs, divers, and even a few professional cave explorers to try and find him but they found nothing. They didn't find a body or any sign of Jack even being there.

Lora cried for what felt like days, drifting in and out of consciousness as she lay in the bright hospital room. She didn't want to eat, didn't want to sleep, and didn't want to respond to any of the questions police and doctors asked. Jenny answered the best she could, but Lora knew now something more was at play here. It was no coincidence. There was more to it and even if she sounded crazy, she had to find out what happened to Jack.

The doctors released her to go home the next day, convinced that her vitals were good. They sent her home with pamphlets as well as the number of the lead detective that was going to look at Jack's disappearance. Lora could barely stay conscious on the trip back to their apartment, Jenny remaining silent the whole drive, only speaking when Lora bust out in tears yet again.

She couldn't believe that mere days after they had finally met, and became intimate, that he was gone. It was all a horrible nightmare and in her weakened stupor, she hoped she'd wake from the dream as she had intended to all along. She half expected to wake up in her bed with Jack's arms around her. Unfortunately, when she did wake up in her bed, she realized only Jenny was there watching over her. This sent her into a fit and the tears were uncontrollable.

Eventually, five days had passed by without a word from the hospital, the detective, or the rescue team. Jenny, whose family had some connections, stayed on top of the search, updating Lora with any news. She also handed over some of Jack's things including his passport. The police had ruled out that he had returned home to the U.S.A. since his passport was still at their apartment. They also eliminated the possibility that he was somewhere else in the country, deciding to skip town or run away. Another excuse, that Jenny clung to, was that he had hit his head and become disoriented and lost.

Jenny had taken personal steps to call every hospital, clinic, and specialist within a 100-kilometer radius of the city to ask about anyone who might fit Jack's description. So far, she had come up empty and the investigators dropped by a week after the incident to inform them that they were giving up the search. No new evidence had sprung up and they had run out of leads.

Lora broke into tears again when they informed her that they had already contacted Jack's family and that arrangements were being made. Jenny held Lora tight as the investigators apologized and told her that if there was anything they could do, give them a call. Of course, Lora still wanted to believe that this was all just a bad dream. Jenny had been the support that held her together that whole week, doing all she could to find out more about Jack's disappearance.

She also took care of the school, explaining the situation to the Dean and the Councilor. She had also hired her own private detective to find out more. Of course, this only worried Lora more. Her friend was doing everything she could to help and all Lora could do was lay around their apartment sobbing over the things he left behind.

It was late at night, two weeks after the incident, that Lora was laying in bed, tears streaming down her face. The deep sadness and loss she felt in her chest and stomach were only compounded every time she looked at a picture of him or saw his bag sticking out from her closet. She frequently slept in one of his shirts until, after two weeks, his scent had faded completely. She was helplessly sobbing on her bed when she heard a set of footsteps outside her bedroom door.

She assumed it was Jenny checking up on her, so she closed her eyes, trying to stop her sobs as her door slowly swung open. She listened in silence as the creaking wooden door swung open. She was about to call out to Jenny when the footsteps started coming closer, another sound accompanying them. Like the sound of dripping and puddling water, slapping on the wooden floor of her bedroom. When she opened her eyes, she almost screamed out in horror. There, standing at the foot of her bed was a ghostly white and green figure of mist and fog.

It was tall, broad, and pale but she could not see its face. It was looking out her window, the familiar shape making her heart drop. When the figure spun around, wildly swaying back and forth, she realized that it was Jack. His eyes were wide, blow green, and his face was sunken and pale. He had dark bags under his eyes and his hand reached out to touch her. She didn't hesitate, lunging forward helplessly at the figure but without luck.

Jack seemed to dissipate as she approached, her hand reaching out to find nothing but mist and moisture on her fingertips. She let the tears fall down her cheeks now as she stood, face to face, with her confused and tormented boyfriend.

"Lora?" he asked, his voice muffled as if he were submerged in water. "Lora, what is happening?"

"Jack," she whispered, reaching out to him. "I'm so sorry…"

"You were drug under," he replied, looking around him now. "I swam after you, but you disappeared. I kicked to the surface but when I could finally feel the air in my lungs, I was drug under again."

"I don't understand," Lora replied, her voice shaking with desperation. She reached out again to hold him but again, he was nothing but mist and moisture.

"I'm trapped underwater between hell and your world," he stated, making Lora muffle her sobs with her hand. "I'm living dead."

"I'm so sorry," Lora whispered through strangled sobs. "It's my fault."

"Forget it, there is a reason, why am I here?" he asked, looking around as if he didn't recognize the room. "I have to see my girls?"

"I don't know," Lora admitted, wrapping her arms around herself. "but…"

"The curse," he echoed, her mouth going dry. "The curse… y-our curse is following you…"

"I don't understand," Lora whispered, her body shaking uncontrollably.

"You know," Jack replied, looking directly into her eyes now. "I am here to warn you, my love."

"Jack," she sobbed, biting her lip in a desperate attempt to muffle her sobs.

"It is coming," Jack continued, his voice becoming distant and unfamiliar. "It killed me, the siren's call will drown out the world. It comes for your soul. Beware the rising river."

"You aren't making sense," she replied, her voice quivering like the rest of her body. "Jack, you're scaring me."

"I'm scared," he echoed, his eyes growing wider still. "It has me and will not let me go. I am doomed by love... I am lost."

"Jack!" Lora cried out, watching as the misty green and white figure started swirling and spinning. Like a cloud of smoke, billowing to the sky, Jack disappeared, evaporating into nothingness. Lora fell to the ground, grasping at the frame of her bed as her body wracked with sobs. A few moments later Jenny came rushing out of her room, standing in Lora's doorway quietly.

Lora didn't care how it looked, crying uncontrollably on the floor as Jenny slowly approached. When she got close, she wrapped Lora in her arms, rocking her gently. Lora didn't even realize it when Jenny had managed to lift her from the cold floor onto the edge of the bed. She didn't even feel the warmth as Jenny hugged her tightly, her own tears streaming down her cheeks.

"I did this," Lora finally sobbed, making Jenny pull back and look at her distressed friend.

"No, you didn't," Jenny said, shaking her head.

"This is all my fault. He died because he loves me. If it wasn't for me, none of this would have happened."

"No," Jenny whispered, her voice becoming quieter with every deep breath. "What do you mean?" Jenny asked, noting the distant look in Lora's eyes.

"The demon," Lora whispered, staring out the window now at the pale moon. "She hunted me, she took Jake, there was a curse, but I didn't understand until now."

"You're not making any sense," Jenny replied, squeezing her friend's arms. "Who hunted you?"

Lora only looked up at her friend with solemn realization, her hands grabbing Jenny's forearms gently. Both girls sat there, staring at one another quietly until Lora finally explains, telling Jenny everything that she's seen in her recent visions and that day in the grotto. Once she is done, Jenny is stunned silent, taking in everything carefully before responding.

"You've suffered an unexplainable horror," Jenny reasoned, watching her friend cautiously. "It is only natural that your mind tries to justify it with whatever it can. I think we should make an appointment with Ursula. She's been calling, asking about you."

"It's not made up, Jenny," Lora pleaded, looking down at her leg where the bruise had been. It had faded already but Lora could still feel the sharp hook that had once been there. "I'm telling you, I'm not crazy."

"No, I don't believe you are," she insisted, pulling Lora into another hug. "But you are hurting. I think you need help and talking to someone about these visions, will allow you to work through your grief."

"You think this is all made up," Lora whispered, feeling more alone than ever. "I'm telling you, there was something in the water with us. There is something more going on and I'm going to prove it."

Lora moved off the bed now, turning on the lamp near her bed before grabbing her laptop. Jenny watched helplessly as her friend started typing away, searching for anything she could find about curses, sirens, and disappearances related to them. Lora didn't even notice when Jenny moved to the other side of the bed, laying down wearily to watch Lora take down notes and bookmark pages and articles.

There was a connection between all of this, Lora knew it. Even if she had to prove it by herself, she was going to make sure she knew exactly why Jack had been taken and where he could be right now. She had to hang on to the hope that he was somehow still alive and that she could figure out a way to bring him back. She had to figure out a way to break whatever curse was holding him, even if that meant making Jenny worry about her sanity.

She found online forums talking about conspiracies and curses, personal blogs of supposed possessions, and a cult webpage about the worship of a water god. She also found legitimate historical records of alleged witch burnings, disappearances, and curses in the middle age up to seventeenth-century that left a scar on the maritime city she lived in. She also found curious charities and dedications to matriarchs of prosperous merchant families who protected their ships and journeys using charms and holy emblems. None of this made any sense to her and soon, everything was blurring together. She was about to give up out of frustration when she stumbled upon something vaguely familiar.

The webpage cited a 2000-year old ritual in which priests would take virgins from royal blood, preform prayers over them, and then send them into the deep or cliffside caves to protect the city's inhabitants from plague, storms, and famine. It didn't mention what happened to the girls, but it did mention an old mariner's tale about sirens and mermaids luring men away from shore and into the caves only to reemerge without a soul. Only when the virgins performed a certain ritual did the souls return to their host bodies. It was all a confusing web and Lora soon became entrenched in pages upon pages of research, references, and books mentioning the same ancient rituals.

Lora didn't even realize that Jenny had fallen asleep next to her or that the sun had started to rise. She had read so many articles and bookmarked so many pages about sirens, curses, and mythology that by the time she had started to feel fatigued, she had over three pages of handwritten notes and over 20 articles and webpages bookmarked. Her eyes had started to sting and before she could stop herself, she shut her laptop, laid back next to Jenny on her pillow, and fell into an uneasy but dreamless sleep.

Lora felt the eyes on her as she wandered through the library, Jenny close behind as she piled her arms full of books. When she had finally found all the ones she had researched online, she had over a dozen titles piled up. She sat quietly at one of the tables in the vast student library, nose buried in chapters about old religious rituals and rights of the Loreley region. After about an hour, she eventually realized that people had started gathering in rows of shelves and other tables around her to stare.

When she looked up at a group of young students only a few rows over, they turned away swiftly, pretending to be in a conversation with one another. Jenny noticed as well, rolling her eyes before turning back to Lora. Lora was confused, eyeing them and the other groups of students around them before Jenny finally grimaced, struggling to explain properly.

"What?" Lora asked, keeping her voice low. "Why are they looking at me?"

"There are rumors around campus," Jenny confessed, rubbing the back of her neck awkwardly. "Some of them aren't so nice."

"Like what?"

"Some freshman think you tried to kill yourself and Jack tried to stop you," Jenny whispered, glancing sideways at the nearest table. "Others think you're suffering some sort of PTSD, though most people are sympathetic."

"People are stupid," Lora grumbled, turning back to her book. Jenny just nodded, biting her lip as she looked at her own book. After realizing Lora wasn't going to let this go, she joined in the research, confident that they would find something to explain all of this. Of course, Lora thought her support was shallow at best, only wanting to keep an eye on her grieving friend.

After another hour of silent reading, with the occasional bout of whispering from other tables and hidden students in rows of books, Lora stood up, gathering a few of them in her bag. Jenny followed, stuffing the others in her bag before following her friend across the hall toward the gallery below. Once they had emerged back onto the campus, Lora quickly walked toward the history department's faculty offices.

"Where are we going?" Jenny asked, watching her friend closely.

"There are a few teachers I'd like to talk to," Lora explained, looking at her phone. "Ingrid Bauman is a reformation and regional history expert here at the university. There is also Karl Schramm, the professor of renaissance literature and history…"

"You think they can help?" Jenny asked, keeping pace with her friend as they approached the entrance to the large brick and wood building.

"If not, they can point me to someone who can," Lora nodded, opening the doors and stopping in the foyer to find out which office they were in.

"They might not be in," Jenny offered, following her friend further into the building toward the elevator.

"Maybe not but it can't hurt to try."

Lora was unsure how to approach the subject with them so decided to focus specifically on the local mythos and religious ceremonies. Doctor Bauman was more helpful that Doctor Schramm. He basically referred her to a few articles and books he wrote, and he also suggested she correspond with a professor from a larger university in a neighboring city. Bauman, however, was more forthcoming, curious about the research Lora was doing considering she was neither a history or theology student.

"Curses and religious ceremonies concerning maritime mythos and superstitions are a very specific research topic," Dr. Bauman, reasoned, looking between the two girls. "Why so much interest?"

"Curiosity," Lora answered before Jenny could explain. "So, tell me, do you know of any regional ceremonies or historical anecdotes that might relate to mythological creatures such as sirens and mermaids?"

"The tales of sirens and mermaids are as old as time," Bauman explained, leaning back in her chair behind the large oak desk. "Ever since the invention of long-ships in the Scandinavia, and even as early as the ancient Greek and Roman civilizations, tales of men being lured to their death by siren songs and mermaid seductions have been prevalent in almost all maritime cultures."

"I'm more interested in specific tales and historical sources about such rituals, and stories from the middle age," Lora explained, becoming impatient. "Do you have any sources or research about those time periods?"

"My research is focused on regional mythology and the reformation and how they intertwined," she explained, watching the two girls closely. "My research is more focused on the religious aspect of locals who had to blend ancient, sometimes pagan ideas with the new, protestant, ideologies."

"And?" Lora asked, pressing her further.

"And, I can think of a few examples of regional religious leaders taking up roles in the ancient rights of seafaring culture," she drawled, considering Lora closely. "Why are you asking, though? You seem to be in a hurry for easy answers but, that is not how history works."

"Professor," Jenny interrupted before Lora could snap back at her. "My friend is desperate for context. She's like a moth in a closet full of linens. She can't help herself when it comes to knowledge. Once she's onto something, she doesn't stop. Can you please indulge her?"

After a long silence, Doctor Bauman nodded, turning from them to the bookshelf behind her, pulling out an older looking tome and opening it. She flipped through a few pages before finding what she wanted, laying the book out on the desk for them to look at.

"This is a contemporary's account of a ritual, performed in the mid-1700s by a protestant preacher," she said, pointing at what looked like a photo-copy of a piece of parchment. It was in a blocky, filigreed font that was hard to read but both Lora and Jenny attempted to decipher it. After they became stumped, Doctor Bauman explained, picking up the book and reading.

"The ritual consisted of a pagan cult, sacrificing a baby of royal blood," she read calmly, not looking away from the page as she continued. "And a procession of a virgin. Once there, the priest would read aloud from the gospels, banishing spirits before taking the blood. For a day and a night their prayers and cries could be heard, echoing from the earth. The priest, after the ritual, would return to the village, where he would bless the people and their endeavors, banishing the call of the evil ghosts for another year. It then goes on to say that this practice was introduced in the region during the late 1300s and dropped out of record in the late nineteenth century."

"What happened after the rituals ceased?" Lora asked, hopeful that this would provide her with some answers.

"Nothing," Doctor Bauman shrugged, setting the book down. "Some villagers carried on the tradition in one sense or another until the outbreak of the first world war."

"But the siren's curse, the rituals, were unique to this region?"

"Yes," she confirmed, closing the book. "Most protestant sects tried to integrate old pagan traditions in various regions to spread the reformation movement. Of course, this led to a wide variety of different rituals."

"But you can confirm, without a doubt, that this particular ritual, this specific regional mythology, was only encountered here?"

"As far as we know," she drawled, sounding a bit impatient.

"Thank you, Doctor," Lora said, nodding her head and standing up. "You've been a big help."

Jenny just looked at her friend curiously before standing as well, following her friend out of the office in a rush. Once they were back outside, hurrying through the center of the busy campus, Jenny grabbed Lora's shoulder, making her stop. The girls exchanged confused looks before Lora sighed, placing a hand on her friend's cheek.

"I'm alright," Lora explained, nodding firmly. "Come on, let's go to our campus stage."

"Are you sure to sing today?" Jenny asked, a bit exasperated. "All the students, profs are there, and only one band will win, the battle doesn't matter, it's important that you're okay!"

"Don't you see?" Lora asked, a wide smile spreading over her face. "My visions, the nightmares, the attack in the cave and in my room the other night. It helped me to finish the song."

"I don't' follow," Jenny said, keeping up with Lora as she started walking back toward the parking lot where her car was parked.

"Come on," Lora nodded, motioning toward the parking lot. "I'll explain everything once we get out of the stage."

"You owe me some lunch," Jenny grumbled, placing her hand on her stomach.

"We can order whatever you want once we got our ticket to the rock battle."

Lora remembered, what she saw at the record session, the anxiety came up again. Jenny always tried to make Lora believe that talking about the tragic incident the whole day, would be worse for her. Jenny promised to never talk about Jack's death. The time was passing by. Girls have to deliver their new song at the campus stage. They were gathering for some hours, playing on guitars and working hard on their new song. Audition day came and they did not even have a recording of it, while other student bands already had thousands of views on youtube.

"We should not go to the audition. They will all laugh about us, we have not even uploaded our song on youtube," Jenny took a deep breath "We have been rehearsing, but on the stage it's live, we are screwed. Let's just go home and start preparing for next year's audition."

Lora answered "No way! We are going to perform! I will not let you sit here and mourn for my dead love all your life."

Jenny stopped, turning to Lora, "Lora, why is it so hard for you to understand, that I will never forget Jack and yes, I will always mourn his death? He was reaching out to help me! And you talk about it like it's only your problem, but no! It's following me too!" Jenny was looking at her eyes and trying to keep calm.

Every time Jenny talked about her and Jack's love Lora felt uncomfortable. Lora put her hand on Jenny's arms and she said with a calm voice "We have to go to the audition. If we don't, RELY will die, just as millions of dreams everywhere do."

Jenny nodded and they moved to the microphones. They were trying to rehearse their song one more time, but Lora's voice was not in good shape.

Jenny disconnected her guitar "I love the piece, we are going to do great on the stage. Just RELY." Lora repeated "Just RELY." and the girls moved to the audition room. Jenny grabbed her notebook, Lora took her e-guitar, Jenny grabbed her bass guitar very fast. They packed more of their musician equipment on the RocknRoller. They stormed out of the door without losing a word. Jenny stopped, thinking after, that she has forgotten something.

Lora moved forward "Let's go, we are most important."

As they moved through the backstage area, Lora saw that the entire hallway was crowded.

Bands are playing their guitar from different corners, everybody's nervous. Lora stared around and for one moment she thought, that she was lost. All the blurry faces were around her. This university. She missed it. Lora loved every professor and every student. It was a place she felt secure. When she was traveling to Germany, she was dreaming of becoming a great rockstar but instead, she became one crazy person with a depressing present and a dark future. Lora was looking to the students who were biting their nails in nervousness, who were laughing overly loud and she only felt peace. That moment Jenny came to Lora putting her palm on Lora's shoulder. They continued their way to the stage.

Lora said to Jenny, "Last panic on the..."

Jenny answered, "We die together, I know"

They run to the sound operator, giving the soundtrack on a flashcard. One of the students spoke to them, "If you show up, then you are the next."

A chaotic mass of students is chilling around applauding the last band that finished their performance. They both grabbed the equipment they needed for live performance then approached the stage.

A voice over the speakers introduced, "Here they are, our next talents, hopefully ready for the upcoming rock battle, two mysterious girls, having something rocky and fresh to share, please welcome RELY on the stage."

The emotions from the audience were mixed. Some homos applauding, some whistling, some

making buh-noise. But when the lighting hit the scene and everybody saw two girls

there was a silence. Everyone was looking at them and wondering what was so deep

and mysterious about the two of them. Most of the rock bands were ignorant boy groups! And now they saw two girls, clothed in dark manga style, sending an aura out, that anyone in the room could feel. The profs stopped to discuss the girls before one of them gave the signal for them to start their presentation.

Lora took the microphone in her left hand, "We decided on a new song that we are still working on, it's like a raw cut we got last night,"

Mr. Miller, Professor of classical music, interrupted her "You still don't have a youtube upload for the piece? Without one, there is no permission, you should know?"

Jenny noped, looking over to him. Then the second professor from media production Ms. Carle said to them both, "To perform on the rock battle you have to upload your video of the recording session very soon." She looked over to her colleges, "It's okay coming up with a new idea, but we don't make the rules, it's the same for all artists."

Mr. Miller asked them, "What is the name and the genre of the piece you want to perform in the battle?"

Lora answered, "We called the song ,Loreley Hill', it's a very wired mixture of genres."

Mr. Miller said, "Ok, let's go."

The room lights go off. Lora and Jenny started to perform, if the beat started. They performed only one part of the song. Lora shut her eyes and began to sing faster once the beat got faster. With every second, she immersed deeper in the rhythm. Everything sounded perfect, combination of the guitar and drums and her indescribably strong and beautiful voice from her inside put her on another level. The notes of the music start spreading around the whole room and people are amazed, they can't get their eyes off of the girls. When the chorus started, the room filled with magical power, a cold wind went through the rows, the people closed their eyes, some raised their hands up, some people lost control of their bodies. They danced unstoppably on Lora's sound. Lora sees her skin change, it grows more, starting from shoulder, over to the left hand. Lora feels the ghost around her coming closer. Something blended in the dark, moving forward to the stage and feels the room. But Lora tries to focus and not to screw her chance anymore. So she closes her eyes and starts singing as strong as she can, as clear as she can and the music is amazing. It just like a wave overwhelming the room. Lora and Jenny in their dark anime outfits are just set stars of the moment, great artists giving the most they can. Once they are finished, the first reaction was silence.

Mr. Miller said something to Ms. Carle, nodding his head with a big pleasance.

Jenny turned to Lora, "It was too much, they don't like it, nobody's making a peep."

The girls started getting nervous. Lora felt her palms getting sweaty and saw the

reflection of the ghost leaving the room, moving between the crowd. She closes her eyes and tries to

convince herself that this is just her fantasy.

Ms. Carle asks the audience, "Any questions from the students?"

The singer from the rock band "White Sons", the band that everyone thought would win, he grabbed the microphone, "I don't wanna comment or discuss the piece," The attention in the room changed with his words. Jenny glared at the boy. "But you never got the things on time, disappearing for weeks, it's better, perhaps you finish the piece, to show up with it next year?"

Some of the students started to make noises at hearing these words. They screamed, "Fuck of

Vince!", but other fans of the White Sons, half of the crowd, started laughing, joking at the girls.

Ms. Carle broke the growing noise, "It's not the case, I like your new song, it would bring some contrast for the battle I think, but think of the big rockstars," She continued, "They have deadlines too, you have to get your record session on time and upload the video to Youtube as fast as possible so we can present your performance to the battle official."

Jenny and Lora were standing on the stage frozen. Lora was relieved, releasing her mixed emotions, while Jenny tried to calm herself and not start screaming to the pretentious Vince and his fans.

Mr. Miller announced, "Next one, please."

Street lights started to glow if Jenny looked out of her apartment window. "I would like two sandwiches," Jenny ordered, before walking to one of the tables and sitting down, placing her bag on the floor with Lora following suit, sitting opposite her.

Lora starred at the sandwiches before her, not only were they unappetizing but disgusting as well.

"I don't want a sandwich," Lora said, staring at the meal in disgust.

"But, you love sandwiches," Jenny replied, looking at her friend with concern. She knew she was going through a hard time and it reflected in everything she did, from the class, apartment, to the studio. "You have to eat something Lora…You haven't eaten a meal in two days," Jenny said, a look of concern on her face.

"I'm not hungry," She said, turning her gaze away from Jenny. She had been so traumatized, nothing enticed her to eat, not even hunger. Her stomach suddenly churned when she spotted a bowl of chicken on one of the tables beside her. "meat…" she said subconsciously, staring at the chicken reducing by the second. She shifted her gaze to the hand reaching out for it, and her hunger from two days suddenly hit her.

"Do you want chicken instead?" She heard Jenny ask, and broke her stare from the bowl. "Really want it that bad?" Jenny chuckled, noticing the spark in her eyes. Picking up tissue from the table, she gently wiped the drool from the side of her lips and ordered a bowl of chicken.

Lora kept stealing glances at the bowl beside her, eyes occasionally making its way to the invading hand. They were huge and fat, fleshier than the chicken. I wonder how they would taste, she thought, confused as to what she was referring to. Her thoughts were interrupted by the meal placed on the table. The smell, the reddish-brown color, and the taste on her tongue. She couldn't get enough of the wonderful feeling as the meat went down her throat and she didn't want the taste to leave her tongue. Everything just wasn't enough.

"Slow down." Lora furrowed her brows in confusion, noticing the look of concern on Jenny's face before looking down. The bowl was almost empty and her palms streaked of oil and pieces of meat. She looked around, noticing the stares from the students in in the camus cafeteria. She quickly ran to the washroom, thoroughly washing her hands and lifted her head. Blue orbs starring back at her and pieces of meat around her mouth. She hastily washed her face before lifting them, a sigh escaping her lips as she saw her usual blue eyes, and she wiped her hands. The light in the room began to flicker accompanied by a light breeze. Lora looked up at the bulb, circling her arms around her body from the cold. Lora quickly looked behind her.

"Hello?" She said in a small voice, looking at one of the cubicle, before slowly walking up to it. Water gently trickled down the white damp door; she could feel its movement down her spine as it slowly traveled. She furrowed her brows in confusion, slowly bringing her hands to touch the door in confirmation but flinched, noticing her palms were dripping wet. A scream emanated from her lips after she turned around.

Red long hair, falling over naked pale skin, dark orbs starring at her from a pale face with traces of green scales. Lora moved back till her back hit the door, still staring at the Image as the atmosphere got dense. She heard humming of music, and blood slowly dripping from the side of the woman's lips. The murmuring soon turned to chuckles as she slowly began to open her mouth, the quantity and pace of the blood increasing. Lora screamed as the woman began to laugh, revealing a set of canine teeth dripping of blood.

"Loreley" She heard the name and the woman disappeared, revealing Jenny standing before her with a look of concern of her face as she held her arms. She looked around, the lights had stopped flickering and the atmosphere was now warm. Everything was back to normal. "What is it?" Jenny asked, holding her shaking friend in her hands with beads of sweat running down her face and eyes wide in fear.

"I-I saw her again, she is a demon… she had blood all over her mouth and s-s-she was laughing, while staring at me through the mirror." Lora stuttered; hand around her body as she looked into Jenny's eyes. Jenny looked at the mirror behind her, before turning her gaze back to Lora.

"Let's go, you need to rest." She said, bringing her into a hug, and took her out of the washroom.

"Every good musician can move the crowd, either physically or emotionally. Whether it's classical, opera, rock…" Lora listened closely while leaning back on the seat, eyes focused on the lecture.

"Do you remember the first time you played that piano, hit those drums, strummed that guitar or any other instrument?" Lora heard the lecturer ask rhetorically, and memories of her first guitar came to mind. She remembered slowly taking it out of the bag, a smile forming on her face, admiring the red color. She remembered the wide smile on his face standing before her, while she thanked him. A smile she looked forward to seeing again with every passing second.

"Lora." Her thoughts were interrupted. She raised her head to see Jenny standing in front of her. "Let's go, It's over." Lora looked around, seeing people leave the hall. She quickly got up from the seat and picked up her bag before walking out the door.

"I'm heading to the studio." Jenny said when Lora took the path towards the apartment. Lora completely forgot about her schedule.

"Oh, yes." She said turning to face Jenny, rubbing her forehead. "We don't have the money for another recording session, do we have any options?" She asked.

"Is it hard to lead a band with a psycho?" Lora asked and Jenny nodded. "It's tough but we have to fight for our dream." Jenny engulfed her in a hug. "I have to show up by dad, you know, our second chance to record, see you tomorrow" She broke the hug and they parted ways.

"When you find anything please tell me." Lora hung up, placing her phone on the night table, before slowly retreating under her blanket. She turned her face and stared at the lamp. She still had hope that Jake would come walking into her arms. She felt her stomach rumble, hunger suddenly hitting her. She stood up, unable to take it and walked to the kitchen. She looked past everything in the fridge until her eyes landed on the packaged fresh meat, and she picked it up. The sight of blood on the meat, made her mouth water. Before she knew it, she tore the foil and began munching the raw meat.

"more…"She said after the meat was done and she threw the packaging away, hastily searching through the fridge. She didn't know why, but all she needed at this moment was more meat. She suddenly heard humming and froze looking through the open door of the kitchen into the bedroom, where she could only see the window and table with her books on them.

"Jenny? "She said, gently closing the fridge and taking slow steps through the kitchen door. She turned to look at her bed, when the lights from the lamp began to flicker. She was walking up to the nightstand when she noticed something odd. She focused her attention on the glass window, seeing the condensation on it, making it translucent. She walked up to the glass, placing her hands around her body from the sudden change in temperature and stared for a while, before turning around to fix the light flicker.

The high pitched laugh and feminine figure with black eyes and blood dripping lips swiftly approaching her was the last thing she heard and saw before everything went pitch dark.

The cacophony of wailing, waves crashing and melodic humming. Everything was dark and there was a restriction to her body movement, the environment felt denser. "Lora", she heard the light whisper of her name. Who's there? She tried to say but the words were stuck in her throat. There was a piercing laugh after a loud crash, and Lora suddenly opened her eyes, panting. She looked around and noticed she was still in her room, lying on the floor beside her bed. She began to cough and felt something try to come out of her throat so she quickly ran to the bathroom, letting out everything in her stomach into the toilet bowl.

"Fuck it." She sighed in exhaustion, getting up from the floor. She yelped, catching a glimpse of her reflection. Mouth and hands buried under a red liquid substance dripping on the floor and traces on her brown pajamas. She slowly brought the substance to her nose, gagging at the metallic scent of blood and the pieces of meat in her nails.

Suddenly the memory of last night hit her. How she munched on the meat in the fridge and collapsed after seeing the vision of that woman. She began to wash the blood of her hands and face, still confused as to why she ate the meat raw and how much blood there is in a raw packaged meat.

The curse had been slowly taking its hold over Lora's body, she noticed it in small amounts at first. It started with her teeth, she had noticed by the way she had accidentally bit down on her lip and blood had poured into her mouth.

As she lifted her lips in her bathroom mirror, the sight of her teeth slowly beginning to curve at the tips into sharp points had her reeling away from the mirror in shock and horror. The skin between her fingers had began to stretch, it was all too similar to the webbing between Loreley's fingers. In shock she looked at her shoulder, barnacles growing on her body. She tried to pluck one of them, making her bleed. Her skin has started to pale.

Walking had become harder, each step as though walking on broken glass, she knew what was happening to her, she was turning into the same monster that had been tormenting her all this time. Her hopes of ending this curse were fleeting, she didn't want to be the same as Loreley, feasting on man's flesh and terrorizing innocent people.

Scarry record session

The star was wake up call for RELY. After the great audition the girls' energy started coming. The battle was coming up and Lora had to have her voice ready for it. Sometimes Lora felt that she was over with her dreams, she wanted to just stop and continue with her life without doing anything but having a boring job, but after not singing for couple of days she felt how she missed playing on the guitar, writing songs and singing them beautifully. Lora decided to not think about the ghost and she started putting all her energy into RELY's success. Lora made some notices at her song text, Jenny came to her, looking over her shoulder.

Lora showed her the chorus idea. Lora had perfected the song in just a few hours and when Jenny read it she could not keep her emotions. "Oh my god! This is genius! You are amazing, Lora! We will do great out there!!!"

While the girls were working on their business, Jimmy the studio helper stormed in, they both ignored him so he turned and retreated. Jenny pressed the export button, they jumped happy and run to the studio staff.

Jenny gave the flashcard to Nic, the chief operator. "We are ready" Lora said, "Sorry for the last

session, we are really ready now."

Chief looked on them without saying a word, he gave the card over to Jimmy with a signal to

insert. Lora continued, "I got the idea for refrain, and Jenny mastered new soundtrack over night."

Chief responded, "You both look great today." he paused.

Neither Lora nor Jenny got what he meant and looked at each other in a confusion. Chief continued, "Yep, I like you guys, but first thing, we have to finish the piece today. You don't wanna loose the money, I don't wanna loose my time, so if we start - no breaks, no tears, no stops, just sing it down, even if the world goes down, just bring it to the end, alright?"

Lora felt little scared after those words but she started thinking about her talent. She was sure that she was ready to record her new song and she was sure that she had something very special, so she nodded, "Yeah

Jimmy started the record on the camera; all installed cameras were recording. Chief made the last move on the mixing pult and pressed the sound record button. His sign to the record room, "Here, we go."

The music started and Lora started to sing. She poured all her emotions into the song. She forced herself not to open her eyes because she knew that something dark may be hiding in the light. Lora only thought about her performance, knowing that she is doing great job. The studio staff liked very much what they were getting, but Nik still concentrated on doing live mixing operations, to perfect the recording process. Jenny looked over to Lora. Lora's voice started trembling and the notes were totally changing. But it was beautifull. Lora lost herself in the performance. She started to perform like a siren. Her voice got stronger and her moves were unusual. Singing the last part of the refrain some energy of the evil ghost filled the studio causing some wind and flickering light, some papers flying away from the desk. Jimmy scared and confused, looking very focused Nik. The recording session is live and shared on Youtube. The live views grow in the beginning from 2k to 27k. Jimmy zoomed the camera view to Lora, not believing his eyes; the light was flickering, short frames of Loras face on the shadowside already mutated to an siren and her eyes lighting in the dark, Jimmy not believing his eyes looked over to Nik again. The performance was meticulous the chief liked it, marking the end. Before Lora stopped to sing their piece again Nik yelled, "Cut. We got it."

Jenny said to Lora "We will win the battle" Jenny jumped over to Lora full of happiness, falling down pulling cables and some equipment with the microphone.

Lora was happy as well but she felt different. Her whole body felt like it had lost all the energy and also gained everything from every single person. Lora was feeling stronger and the weaker at the same time. This feeling was unknown and weird to her.

Chief said to Jimmy with a huge smile on his face, "Because of that, I love this job."

Jimmy answered with a surprised face, "Did you see that?"

Chief turned his head to him, "Of course, most important, I had heard, go and check the electrical box, I have to check the record file."

Lora and Jenny looked over to the chief. He activated his voice in the cabine. "Great guys, you got 39 thousand live previews already on Youtube, the file is in safe, I am proud of you," he said, laughing but he stoped laughing looking at the videofile: In the clip dark areas is something mystic is moving around like a dark figure, you can see it only mirrowing the picture upside down. He looked over to Lora on the screen, not believing his eyes; Lora's skin was shining and sparkling. Her pale face looked scary. Lora saw the problem too mirroring in glass. Lora gets frightened of her own self and before she burst out in tears, she rushes out of the room. Jenny followed her screaming, "Lora stop!"

Jimmy and Chef were confused not realizing what just happened. They look at each other muted. Finally Chef manages to say few words, "Don't ask, I don't know, but the song is a hit, this is sure."

"I have to do something, or I'm gonna be a real psycho." Lora looked at Jenny across the table, flipping through the book.

"It couldn't be your trauma presenting itself in a different form." Jenny said, raising her head from the book to stare at her friend. "I'm not expert on this, but we almost drowned a week ago," she sighed "and Jake is still...missing," she added, making sure to use the right words.

The mere mention of his name was like a stab in the chest. If he hadn't gone back into the water, he would have been here with her.

"How did you get out of the water?" Lora asked, looking down at her open book. "He jumped in to save you." she said, pain building up in her chest.

"Lora, I said..."Jenny started to reply, looking at her friend.

"If we had been careful...He would still be here." Lora said, staring blankly at the page.

"They will find him." Jenny assured, knowing that's the only thing that could calm the anger building up.

"Sorry." Lora apologized, lifting her gaze from the book. "It's not your fault."

"Let me get you some water, you look pale."Jenny got up and went to the kitchen. Lora placed her elbow on the table and rested her head in her palms, looking down at the page. She tried hard to focus, but her mind keeps shifting to Jake. She spotted a drop of water on the page, then another. Brows furrowed in confusion, she raised her head and noticed her palms dripping wet.

"Lora." She heard a whisper of her name and looked behind her.

"Jenny?" She called out. She turned her gaze, noticing the flicker of the light from the kitchen.

"Jenny?"She heard the familiar humming and she slowly approached the doorway. She screamed, terrified by the scene before her. The same woman squatted, munching on Jenny's limp body. Her friend's eyeball hanging out of the right socket, jaw bone showing under torn bloody flesh with blood streaming down to the floor. She suddenly turned, black eyes glowing, blood staining her face and exposed canine teeth, black scales covering the lower half of her body and an erect snake fin traveling down her spine. Lora began to move back, shaking intensely as the humming got louder. The creature swiftly crawled towards her and Lora screamed, covering her face from the approaching claws.

"Lora." She slowly opened her eyes to reveal Jenny looking at her with concern and a glass of water in her hand. Lora looked around, standing in front of the doorway to the kitchen. Everything was in order.

"What's wrong?" She returned her gaze to Jenny.

"She…you…blood." Lora managed to say, amidst her shaking voice.

"You need help," Jenny said, leading her to the couch. Jenny grabbed the phone and moved to balcony speaking with Ursula.

Lora walked into the bedroom, threw her bag on the bed and hurriedly sat at the study table placing the book on it. She flipped through the pages until her eyes landed on the word.

"Loreley." She said. Red hair falling over naked body, harp in her hand, pale scaleless skin glowing under the sunlight as she sat on a huge rock.

"Lora." She stopped reading and turned her head to her side. Water dripping from his blond hair, causing some of the locks to stick to his pale face, hosting green eyes that stared at her.

"Jack?" Lora said, slowly getting up from her seat, still staring at him. A smile formed on his face. Lora launched forward and engulfed him in a hug. "I knew you'd come back to me, I knew it." Lora sobbed on his shoulder. "I'm so sorry; I shouldn't have let you jump in that water." She said, feeling arms circle around her back.

"It's okay, swallow." She heard the deep voice of her boyfriend, which had gotten deeper. She broke the hug to look at his face, water trickling down to his drenched white shirt and brown shorts.

"Let me get you a towel." Lora tried to leave but he held her in place, holding her hands in his, not breaking eye contact. More sobs escaped her lips. "I miss you."

"I love you," Jack said.

"I love you more," Lora said, a wide tragic smile forming on her face. "Where were you all this time?" Lora brought her hand to cup his wet cheeks.

"I've been in your heart," Jake said, still looking into her eyes.

"Listening to your song," He continued. Jack sat down on the sofa as if everything was back to normal. Lora leaned towards him and laid her hand on his wet neck. Jack with a smile on his face, "All the girls waited for me for nothing, I saw how the snails had eaten them away."

Lora waited for a moment, enjoying seeing him again, "You cared about that more than about me?"

"I want to play for you like we always do," Lora said, removing her hand from the grip and hastily walked up to the guitar.

Lora smiled and began to sing the beginning of her new song. She noticed his smile widen and the grip on her hand tighten.

"The first so…" There was no one there. Lora turned. "Jake?" She called out, looking around the room. "Where are you?" She walked to the kitchen but found no one. "Guess you want to wipe up the water." She walked towards the bathroom after she heard Jenny's voice.

"Come on, Ursula was able to squeeze us in tonight for an emergency session," Jenny explained, rubbing Lora's shoulder gently. "I've got food already delivered. I got you some salad, that rice you like, and a good assortment of fruit. It's been a while since we've had a balanced meal."

Lora just nodded, placing her guitar back. She sat up slowly, rotating her head to get rid of the stiffness in her neck. She really needed that nap, looking at her phone and realizing she'd not slept for almost two days. Jenny just smiled, hopping up off the bed and sauntering out into the hallway. Lora followed groggily, rubbing her eyes before realizing that Jenny had laid out a buffet for both of them on the countertop. There was rice, mixed vegetables, fruit, two different kinds of chicken, an assortment of random pastries, and wine.

Lora didn't realize how hungry she was until she spotted all this food, making Jenny grin as she dug right in, filling her plate with rice, fruit, vegetables, and all sorts of dishes. Both girls sat comfortably at their coffee table, Lora opting to sit on a cushion on the floor to enjoy their feast. It was only when they had devoured almost all their food that Jenny poured them another glass of wine each. Lora put the food aside. She ran into the bathroom and puked everything out.

"What's wrong? Should I cancel on Ursula, she said she can come here to meet with us," Jenny said, handing her friend the glass of water. "She'll be here at seven. I didn't want this to feel formal to you like you were in her office or something. It is a more intimate setting."

"Thank you, I'm okay." Lora smiled, taking a sip of the glass. "I think I'd have become worried and probably would have wanted to back out if we had to make the drive across town."

"It's not a problem at all," Jenny chuckled, drinking some of her wine. "Ursula is a professional, but she did agree that an informal session in the comfort of your own home might make it easier to deal with the trauma we are going through."

"You didn't tell her about our theory, did you?" Lora asked, looking at the papers and books that had been neatly stacked on the side table. She noted that Jenny left the corkboard and whiteboard up on the wall.

"No, but she'll want to know," Jenny offered, leaning back on the couch slowly.

"As I said, she'll just think I'm using this conspiracy as some sort of coping mechanism," Lora replied, remembering her last session with Ursula. "She told me I was using Jack like that, to get over my insecurities and validate myself."

"She's just here to help," her friend warned, sitting her glass of wine down.

"Fine, but I won't speak of the curse," Lora retorted, watching her friend closely. "I refuse to be told that it is all made up, in my imagination or whatever. I won't do it."

"Fine," Jenny conceded, raising her hands in defeat. "But she knows her job. She's going to figure out something is going on."

"I'm not sure she will," Lora sighed, leaning back on the couch.

There was then a knock at their front door, Jenny standing up swiftly to answer it. Lora straightened herself as best she could, standing up to greet Ursula as she stepped into their small foyer.

"I'm glad you called," Ursula told Jenny, a pleasant smile on her face. She turned to Lora now. "I see you've got some wine."

"I'll get you a glass," Jenny offered, turning to the kitchen with a nod. Lora smiled, offering for Ursula to come into the living room. After she took a seat on the couch, Jenny came in with an empty glass, setting it on the coffee table and pouring the wine.

"Thank you," Ursula nodded, taking the glass in her fingers and taking a sip. "So, how have you been holding up, Lora?"

"I'm devastated," Lora admitted, keeping her voice calm. "I loved him and to lose him like I did broke my heart."

"You seem quite calm about it," Ursula commented, leaning back into the couch. "How are you processing the grief?"

"Gradually," Lora replied, leaning forward and grabbing her own glass of wine. "I take it day by day until it starts to get easier."

"Mature of you but you seem on edge," Ursula replied, watching Lora closely. "Are you nervous?"

"This is all new to me," Lora assured, taking a drink of her wine. "I have no idea how to properly handle something like this and I don't really know how to discuss this with a therapist."

"So, you're worried about how I might judge you?" Ursula questioned, her voice calm.

"It's your job to judge and analyze people," Lora reasoned, setting her glass back down.

"Sometimes," she agreed, leaning forward. "But my job is to enforce healthy outlets and understanding of human emotion and how it affects our lives."

"And you think I'm not handling this in a healthy way?" Lora asked, becoming irritated.

"I'm not judging you," Ursula assured, glancing at Jenny.

"What did she tell you?" Lora asked, not missing the look they exchanged.

"I'm worried about you," Jenny admitted, her voice full of indignation and fear. "You're suffering and I didn't know what else to do."

"She only told me her side of the story," Ursula reassured, looking between the two girls. "So, what is your side?"

"You'll just think I'm psychotic or delusional," Lora spat, glaring over at Jenny. "This is why I didn't want to talk to her about this."

"She's not going throw you into an asylum or something," Jenny replied, hurt by Lora's response.

"Please, elaborate more on the curse," Ursula urged, folding her hands on her lap in a professional manner.

"Don't you understand?" Lora asked, looking back at the older woman. "I don't know what it is about – I'm lost. I just know that it isn't a coincidence. It can't be."

"So, you've seen this in your visions, before he even came to visit?" Ursula questioned, observing the other two.

"Yes, and then I saw it again that day, when he disappeared," Lora urged, standing up now. "I've tried to find anything and everything I could about this, but nothing is adding up. I'm missing a piece…"

"Lora," Jenny urged, standing up now. "We've been at this for days, trying to figure it out, and nothing is making any sense. You're drawing parallels that don't exist and you are starting to become obsessed. It's not healthy!"

"I thought you trusted me," Lora accused, turning to her friend in a rage. "You know me! You know I wouldn't make something like this up. You've seen the evidence, the rituals, the news articles and records of disappearances in the past fifty years. You know there is something going on!"

"I think we need to stop and reassess," Ursula interjected, standing now. She walked over to them now, placing a hand on Jenny's shoulder gently. "Lora, Jenny is worried about you and though she may see some parallels in all of this, she doesn't believe that it is the main issue. The main issue for her is your wellbeing."

"You know I would never do or say anything to hurt you," Lora said, looking at Jenny solemnly. "But I know I am right."

"And your need to justify Jack's death," Ursula continued, making Lora glare at her.

"He's not dead," Lora hissed, feeling the anger boiling in her stomach.

"He is dead, Lora," Ursula pushed, her voice still calm and sympathetic. "He is gone, and you cannot accept that reality. That is why you are pushing for justification, for a reason why all of this has happened to you. I can assure you, it isn't because of some curse or religious ceremony. Things like this aren't predictable and that uncertainty is something you don't want to face."

"You haven't seen the things I've seen," Lora insisted, her voice becoming harsh, full of anger. She couldn't control it, all her rage coming to a head here and now. She had a feeling this is what Ursula had intended, to give her an outlet to vent, but she couldn't accept it. She couldn't believe that Jack was truly gone, and she wouldn't accept that there was nothing she could do about it. There was no reason, no connection between him and such a harsh and final death. She was going to get him back, even if that meant she had to do it alone.

"We're just trying to help you," Jenny insisted, trying to calm her friend down.

"No, you're just trying to get me to accept that the love of my life is dead for no reason other than pure coincidence and bad luck," Lora spat, the bubbling rage within soon overflowing into sparks of venom and fire. "I won't accept that!"

"Death is inexplainable," Ursula reasoned, stepping closer as Lora mirrored her with a step back. "You cannot justify and explain every tragic death in this world. It is impossible, no matter which way you approach it."

"He's not dead!" Lora insisted, clenching her fists so tight that her nails were digging into her palm. "He lives!"

"He's gone," Ursula offered, her voice becoming softer, almost patronizing.

"Please, Lora," Jenny whispered, watching her friend helplessly. "I'm worried about you…"

"And I'm worried about Jack," Lora spat, rounding on Ursula who had taken another step closer. Lora didn't know what came over her, feeling the anger within jump, like an uncontrollable tug on an invisible string. Before Lora knew what she was doing, she had lunged at Ursula, letting out a shrieking, almost deafening scream that echoed about them. Jenny covered her ears, watching her friend in mute horror.

Lora could see, as if peering from within, her hands reaching for Ursula's neck, but they weren't her hands. They were long, knotted, pale, and crooked with blackened claws that reached out, instinctually clasping tightly around the older woman's pale, slender throat. Lora moved with horrifying speed and indifference, the rage within her overriding everything as she felt the life crush beneath her fingers.

Jenny let out a frightened scream, Lora's eyes snapping to her in the foggy haze of fury and adrenaline. She then screeched, unconsciously bellowing a horrific noise, echoing like thousands of birds chirping all at once. Jenny looked pale, sickly, reaching out to catch herself on the counter as she backed away. She was trying to flee, Lora's hands reaching out to grab at her but before her claws had sunk into Jenny's back, her friend collapsed. She fell onto the floor with a thud, her body becoming stiff and still, as if she was paralyzed.

There was another tug, Lora's stomach turning as she fled, her movements quick and graceful as if she were floating on air. She moved past Ursula's twisted body to the large glass window, opening it with a hiss. She then reached out, grasping the railing of their small balcony and jumping, headlong into the open air with a harrowing shriek. It drowned out the sound of passing cars three stories down, the blare of horns, sirens, and voices as she fell, the ground rising fast to meet her.

She thought she would lose consciousness, feeling herself floating as if suspended on an ocean of air. She then realized that she was already on the ground, looking through hazy eyes at the world around her. It had become grotesque, dark, horribly mangled and full of bright, pulsing hot lights. She wanted to shield her eyes and felt her dry, tight skin start to ache. She didn't understand, instinctually rushing across the lawn toward the river.

She didn't know what she was looking for, but the pain was insatiable, a burning that started to sink into her skin. She writhed in pain as she searched around in the dark for a reprieve. She moved, almost without thought, gracefully speeding past parked cars and the highway, not even bothering to look for traffic as she crossed to the sidewalk and buildings on the other side. She couldn't control herself, couldn't stop as hunger began to grow within her. Everything was moving so fast and before she knew it, she had cornered a young college student in the dark alley between the library and the labs.

He looked at her with mild disgust, his eyes growing wide when she reached out, digging her claws deep into his neck and shoulder. She was hungry, lustful for his blood as her own horribly sharp teeth sunk into his flesh. She could feel his warm, metallic blood dripping from the corners of her mouth as she gnawed, sucked, and ingested all he had to offer. The sensation of her claws and teeth buried in his flesh was the most exhilarating thing she'd ever felt, and she couldn't believe what she was thinking. She was losing herself to this anger, to this feeling of utter rage and injustice and it had transformed her into this horrific creature called a siren

Lora woke in a drunken haze, her head splitting as she tried to regain her senses. The first thing she realized is that she wasn't at home. She was trying to sit up, to gain her senses and the rock formation came into focus, the sound of waves close by as she noticed that the sun was rising. She felt cold and realized that her skin felt cakey, almost completely dried out. She looked down and realized that the outfit she was wearing was torn to shreds, hanging off of her like rags over her muddied and bruised skin.

When she looked closer, the surrounding becoming brighter, she saw that the dark blotches on her skin weren't bruises or mud.

The color was off, dried and scarlet with brown tints. She gasped as the memories came flooding back. Her body was trembling, remembering every face as she tore her claws and teeth into supple muscular flesh. She was horrified, the flashes of gore, blood, and rage coming back to her all at once.

She had strangled Ursula, remembering the feel of her small neck under her long, crooked fingers. She also remembered Jenny, her stomach turning as she coughed and wretched into the dirty ground covered in seaweed, kelp, and stones. Jenny had fallen to the ground, unconscious and paralyzed and Lora worried that something might have happened to her. She had flown into a rage last night and didn't understand what had happened. She tried to catch her breath, calming herself so she could take in her surroundings. Lora swiftly sat up straight, panting, looking around and noticed she was sleeping outdoor, on the rock beside her residence. The metallic smell of blood evaded her nose.

She stood up slowly, feeling her weak legs under her as she stepped toward the rickety door. She saw a decaying dock, noticing that she was along the stony edge of the river coast, against the rocks and cliffside caves.

There was no one around, the sound of rushing water, and wind overpowering any voices or ships that might be close by. She had no idea where along the coast she was at and was worried that soon, she would be found and taken in for murder. She felt her stomach sink, vomit spewing out onto the ground as she lunged forward to her knees. It was rough, her stomach turning and her throat burning as she wretched up bloody mucus and flesh, the taste metallic and rotten.

The smell was unbearable; the fish mixing with the acidic metallic blood didn't help her stomach.

She tried to stand up but her legs were still weak as she stared out over the foaming gray and green waves along the beach. She didn't know what she could do or what she should do. She had murdered someone innocent, several people who were innocent, and she didn't have any excuse or reasoning for her untamed and vicious actions. She was unhinged, wrapping her arms around herself fearfully as she rocked back and forth.

Gagging at the foul taste in her mouth, she ran into apartment to the bathroom and emptied her stomach into the toilet bowl.

She tiredly walked out in her bathrobe, headed to her bed but turned to the door after she heard a knock. She opened the door to reveal Jenny in her usual black shirt and shorts.

"What is it?" Lora asked, noticing the sorrowful look on her face.

"Three refugees were found dead this morning."Jenny entered the room and sat on the couch. "The same thing happened three days ago…Their faces were torn to shreds."

"Just like my vision," Lora said to herself, staring at Jenny with a blank expression.

Jenny continued "We have to perform tonight. Let's go to the lecture." She said.

After the lecture, Lora went very hastily to her apartment. She didn't feel well, she didn't know if it was the nervousness before the performance or the inhuman hunger.

Her eyes were wide with panic as she watched the water pour from the walls, a sight that had become so ingrained in her mind that it no longer seemed unusual. Trembling from her stiff position in the center of the room, the young woman cried out as she was shoved roughly from behind by an unseen force.

Stumbling forward from the rough push, she wasn't given so much as the chance to fall. The firm grip that had once left the nasty bruises on her shoulder, wrapped around her wrists equally as tightly as they had that day.

Brutishly, she was dragged, thrown against the wall of her bedroom right by the door leading to the bathroom. Eyes squeezed closed, the young woman wheezed as the wind was knocked out of her. Weak body slumping to the ground, there were no brief moments of peace, no seconds of solace, there was simply pain.

The unseen force reached down to grab fistfuls of the young woman's hair, dragging her along the tiled floors into the bathroom by her scalp. Lora was dragged through a puddle of water, the walls were overflowing, the entire room was drenched.

Her bathtub filled so high, water began to spill off of the edges, only adding to the collecting pool on the ground.

Lora cried out in pain as she was yanked up, forced onto her knees and spun to face the bathtub. Weakly, she grasped onto the edge of the porcelain tub tightly, squeezing her eyes closed and gasping in a panicked breath before her head was forced into the tub and under the copious amounts of water.

Her legs kicked and thrashed at the water coating the ground, hands reaching up to her head to try to push and claw at the hand holding her under. Eyes squeezed closed and fatigued lungs burning, the last of the air she had taken in floated from her mouth in bursting bubbles.

The spirit moved away from Lora when the lamps stopped flickering. Exhausted and frightened, Lora spat the water out of her mouth and collapsed on the floor. At that moment her mobile phone rang.

She heard the voice of her family doctor "You wanted to come by, I have time today".

Lora coughed again and replied, "I need your help, I'm coming over."

As soon as she had received the call, the young woman got herself together and got up, grabbed her bag and was out the door within minutes. Lora didn't bother calling an Uber, she didn't bother waiting for a taxi to come around. She had raced out of the door and sprinted the entire way to the doctor's office, despite the pain in her legs, despite the distance, she just had to get there.

Panting and covered in a thin sheen of sweat, Lora finally sat in the chair in her doctor's office. The man appeared quite dubious at her words, even more so when he saw the way she was fidgeting. He pinned it down to possible drug use or even a psychotic episode.

The doctor had ordered a blood test to make sure that she wasn't on a dangerous amount of illegal highs. Lora had agreed within an instant, thinking that perhaps it could answer some questions, give her some kind of clarity.

The male wiped the inside of her elbow, she didn't even flinch as he pushed the needle into her skin. She had been in so much pain over the last few weeks with the ordeal of the curse that the pinprick was nothing to her.

She sat back against the table, her brows furrowed, a hand settled on her stomach. The sweat on her brow didn't seem to be from her run anymore, now it seemed to be more of a cold sweat, wearing a face of discomfort.

As the doctor pulled the syringe out of her arm and turned around with the vial in hand, slowly approaching his desk so he could scribble down the details. Lora's head turned to face him slowly, her lips parted as she panted shakily.

As she stared at her doctor's back, she was overcome with a sudden feeling of intense hunger. Her gums ached with desire, it was like her brain was telling her to stop but her body simply wouldn't comply. Panting shakily as she slowly slipped off of the medical table, trembling hands reaching out towards him.

"Lora--"

She didn't give the man another second to speak, her hand stretched out, covering his face with her fully webbed fingers, the sharp claws on the tip of her nails digging into his face. Leaning forward, her sharp, pointed teeth on display as she stretched her jaws open, clamping down on the man's shoulder.

The male screamed against her palm, the sound of his excruciating pain muffled against her hand. The skin on her hand was glowing, much like Loreley's used to when Lora saw her in her visions.

The taste of his blood on her tongue was the best that she had ever experienced, a crazed haze clouding her mind as she bit down. Sharp fangs dragging through muscle and tendon, as her teeth met, the man writhing in agony in her arms fell limp. He dropped to the floor in a slump, lifeless body leaking crimson blood all over the floor.

Even as she chewed the raw flesh with unnerving squelching sounds, blood pouring down her chin, she was still beautiful. Blank eyes glowing a bright fluorescent shade, gulping down her mouthful, she took a shaky breath, glancing down at the doctor by her feet before she hurriedly dropped to her knees to continue her meal.

The rock battle

Rock battle night finally came. Lora had been rehearsing a lot. Their video had thousands of views and many people were predicting that RELY was going to be a winner of this year's battle.

The rock battle is on the track-stage. Up to 1000 fans and rock junkies all around. Some Simson bikers are making on noise. White Widow Sons band is performing. The people like their music and the gothic converse styled and white-clothed guys. At the performance it is screened, how much live followers are on Y-outube. At the end of the performance the jury presents the highest stand of likes after preview. So the online live viewers decide whos song and the band was the best.

The jury informs the winner will be a part of the big open-air festival. Up to the previous bands White Widow Sons gathered the most likes. To no surprise, they could be the winner. They were the only real enemies of RELY.

Now it was time for RELY's performance. The jury presents the Youtube stars the mysterious band received. "RELY" . Lora grips the mic "this song is for my love, for my dead love" she smiles softly and produces a wonderfull e-guitar noise. After that the beat starts according to Jennys wonderfull bas-G performance and live drummer just a third drummer girl of the camp.

The fans are excited, near to refrain the dark cloud is approaching the place, the light effects starts flickering. People have gotten extase state, Lora's eyes glow, Youtube views double and reach a million live views. The triple of the former band. Lora is singing beautifully and also scarily. She is running on the stage, pouring her heart and all her energy into the song. The song is so strong there the heaven flickers too. A storm is near. Wind and rain starts. Some people start running to the exit, but others are mesmerized by this beautiful song, so they just continue dancing. RELY finish the performance. The Jury wanders with standing ovations. The mass follows and making a beat out of the ovations. All looking the time runner. It's only one minute time to gather the likes on Youtube, the same procedure every band before got through.

One of the juries is smiling in amazement. He is the one who has to announce the number of likes. He looks into the phone and says with strong voice: "3,2,1. So with 198017 likes. The winner is RELY." People start ovations of happiness. They are all in nirvana and they act like RELY's music is a narcotic for them. Their eyes are shining and their skin is bright, they clap and clap, like robots. Lora looked over them smiled and bowed her head as a symbol of thanks. This gesture caused louder ovations. The jury continues talking in the microphone while people are going wild in the background. "You got the trophy and you can perform on the real rock stage in front of thousands."

Somebody takes the trophy on the stage and Jenny is the one who grabs it. She is waving at people then she looks around to find her partner but Lora is not there anymore. Jenny starts searching for her. Jenny runs down into the side scenes and sees Lora running to the exit. She was trying to escape the place. „Stop!" she screams and follows her. "Lora, please stop!"

She starts begging and Lora stops. She is breathing heavily from running and she leans on her knees. „Jenny, I'll die... I feel like I'm already dead... Jenny, you have to tell me everything, please... Tell me what happened that night." Jenny saw tears in Lora's eyes.

„Okay, I promise I will tell you everything." Jenny smiles at Lora and hugs her, „but before we both have to get to some party and get the heads pumped." Lora agreed, without losing words.

Jenny feels like their dream is coming true and this feeling made her like a zombie. No feelings no emotions. Lora tries to understand, if it is her talent at all, or it is the siren using her body to sing.

Lora got out of the stage, vigorously wiping her hair and walked to place her guitar into the case. "Jack?" She said, after lifting her head to see him standing across on the other side of the crowded room, clothes and hair still soaking wet. Lora walked around the crowd and engulfed him in a hug. "Where did you go?... Why did you leave? ...Please don't leave me again…" Lora choked on sobs.

"It's okay," Jack said, wrapping his hands around her. Lora broke the hug to look at his pale face.

"You need to clean yourself up, you will catch a cold. Remember you hate colds." Lora smiled.

"I love you," Jack said, taking her hand into his, not breaking eye contact. " The demon called Loreley has attacked us because we love, so now I am living dead but trapped in her hell."

"I love you more, babe," Lora replied, another tear falling down her cheeks. "That's why I waited for you, and you came back."

"I've always been in your heart," Jack said. "Can you sing for me again?" He added, the grip on her hand getting tighter. Lora smiled.

"I wrote this song and it's only for you," Lora said, removing her hand from the grip to pick up her guitar. He sat down next to her.

"It's only you…" Nobody stood there after Lora raised her head. "Jack." She called out, looking to her side but there was no response. She stood rooted to the spot, staring at where he stood. There was a knock on the door and Lora quickly turned her head, a smile forming on her face. "Jack." She happily opened the door and her smile slowly died down.

"We did it." Jenny walked past her into the room. "Look at this." She said, handing her phone to Lora.

"Number one on every chart." Jenny squealed "200 million views in two days. We've been all over the news thes… " Jenny stopped, noticing the blank look on Lora's face.

"He was here, Jack was here," Lora said and Jenny's smile disappeared.

"Lora, you scare me, you have to let him go." Jenny sighed in frustration.

"He came, and spoke to me…"

"He's dead," Jenny shouted. "He drowned in the water and died…Everything is in your head." She calmed down, noticing the pained expression on her face. "Sorry," She said, and slowly brought her into a hug. "He's dead, stop listening to me, and yourself." Jenny broke the hug, furrowed her brows in confusion while looking at the blank expression on Lora's face, as she started humming. "Hey." She placed her hand on her cheeks, the humming got louder and her skin got cold. Jenny shook her by her shoulder and she broke out of her trance, blinking severally.

"I have to go," Lora said and quickly changed her outfit.

"You have to go?" Jenny asked, as Lora walked past her and left.

News had spread amongst the townspeople, the strange phenomenon that had recently been occurring. When the tides would rise, people seemed to go missing, it was thought to be the dangers of the sudden rush of incoming water.

It was written off as a natural disaster, a simple accident that unfortunately took the lives of unsuspecting victims. That was, until they found the first body, washed up ashore. One of the victims of the so-called 'accident'.

His cause of death?

As if the bite marks and scratches covering every inch of the young man's body weren't enough of a telltale sign, it was clear to see that this wasn't a natural disaster in the slightest.

Lora, to her peers, didn't appear any different. She attended her classes, spent time with her girlfriend Jenny occasionally, and everybody loved her new song.

Lora had recently sought out the help of the residing priest, the only hope she had left in her situation. After hearing her troubles, he didn't hesitate to pin down her issues to the haunting of an evil spirit which had attached itself to her.

"She lures them by her song, makes their boats crash on the rock and watches them drown. She lost her love in water, afraid he was cheating on her." The old priest said. Dark circles around his eyes hosting pale pupils, gray hair falling on the side of a face that looked creepy under the candlelight. "She never left, her spirit still lives there," he said. "Looking for the right vessel."

"Why is she hunting me?, how do I stop this?" Lora asked desperately.

"She doesn't hunt...Our thoughts are her Strength." Priest said.

To remedy this, he had summoned her back to the church after the sermon and everyone had left, so they could perform an exorcism in peace.

She knelt upon the steps leading up to the altar, head bowed and hands clasped together. The priest stood before her, in his hand, a bottle of holy water, and in the other was his on hand bible. Kneeling before the Lord with a man she believed would offer her protection, she felt a serene sense of peace.

Though it was a peace that she knew wouldn't last.

The evidence of that fact?

The water that was slowly pouring down the steps, soaking the knees of her jeans right the way up to her thighs.

The priest's reciting of the bible came to a sudden halt, the sounds of his loafers squelching as they filled with water, his confused mumbles as he stepped around in the water.

"Did the holy water spill?" She could hear him mumbling.

Lora said nothing, squeezing her eyes closed tighter, clenching her hands together firmer.

"H-huh? What's that? Begone demon! How dare you step foot in the house of God!"

She could hear the male slowly stumbling in the water, fear laced thick in his voice. It didn't take long for the cry of pain to reach her ears, the sound of the agonizing scream and fluids pouring onto the floor below.

Lora didn't waste another second, while Loreley was busy with the priest, she raced out of the church doors. Her shoes slapping against the layer of water covering the marble floors as she burst through the door and down the steps to get as far away as possible.

What disturbed her most about the whole ordeal, however, was just how good it smelt when Loreley had split that poor, innocent man in two.

She was disgusted in herself, with the way her stomach rumbled at the mere thought of getting a taste of the flesh that Loreley had just devoured. She shuddered uncomfortably as she glanced down at her stomach, it had begun to churn with uncomfortable hunger pains, she needed to eat, and not any ordinary type of food.

The young woman's head snapped up, her crisp eyes lost in the glowing, monstrous gaze left behind. Licking her lips slowly, she raced down the street towards the docks, she was always drawn to the water when the need to feast arose.

When she had made her way down to the docks, the sounds of loud voices, cheer and laughter had caught her ear. Glowing irises turning towards the source of the noise, it was a shock, tied to the pier. It appeared to be the source of an ongoing party, standing on the pier beside the ship, were a few young men as well as a police officer, most likely there to guard the high profile members attending the party.

Hearing so many voices, smelling so much blood come together in one group ripe for the picking, she couldn't contain herself.

Swiftly, Lora marched her way towards the ship, towards the men who stood around outside with alcoholic beverages in hand. As they saw the beautiful young woman approach, the men snickered to themselves, gently nudging one another with their elbows as though expecting her to come on to one of them.

What they got, however, were no flirtatious remarks. Rather, they were met with a gaping jaw filled with razor-sharp fangs, she took out the black young men first, still smart enough in her ravenous hunger. Her sharp teeth clamping down on his jugular, tearing his throat clean from his body in a matter of seconds.

The other men stood stunned, jaws gaping as they watched the young woman spit out part of the police officer's vertebrate. A bloody grin spread wide across her face, she charged at the unsuspecting group, tackling them all into the water with a surprising display of strength. In her domain, where she could display the best of her strength, the men weren't given a chance. All that rose to the surface after her vicious attack was a bubbling pile of fresh, leaking blood.

The smell of blood evaded her nose and she slowly removed her hand from her hair. She stared in horror, palms covered in blood with pieces of flesh in her nails. The laugh echoed through the room and Lora quickly ran out. She kept running till she arrived at a river and hastily washed her hands and face, shaking intensively.

Every splash of water was a crash of wave to her, the wailing, humming, everything was getting loud and her body getting cold under the moonlight.

"That's Lora..."

"Her song is a bop…"

"Wish I could sing like her…"

"She lost her boyfriend a month ago…"

"Where are her clothes…"

"She looks pale…"

"I think she still can't get over it… " Lora heard as she walked briskly towards her apartment, clutching tightly on her sweater with her head bent, ignoring the stares from people.

"It's a monster…it's her, I saw it." Lora turned and saw a boy sitting on the floor in front of the apartment building, white shirt covered in dirt, shaking intensively with beads of sweat falling down his face. "She was eating them." He said, staring around nervously while a crowd slowly formed around him. Lora ran quickly into the apartment building as people began to recognize her. She was about to open her door but froze for some seconds before going upstairs. She knocked on the door, looking around nervously.

"You look horrible," Jenny said, opening the door for her friend. Lora walked to the couch, still clutching her sweater and sat down. "Why are you so pale?... and your clothes are very striking.", Jenny sat beside her.

"Do you think I'm a monster?" Lora asked, turning to look at her friend.

"No, you are not," Jenny said. "You're in pain." She held her hands and squeezed tightly. "I will help, you get yourself together." Jenny got up and went to get a glass of water from the kitchen. "We have a show tonight." She said, handing the water to her.

"Lora…Lora" Lora quickly opened her eyes and looked around the room. She slowly got up from under the blanket, staring at the figure in front of the bed

"Jack!" she walked towards him and gently placed her hands on his wet cheeks. "Why do you keep leaving, everyone thinks you're dead," Lora said, staring into his green eyes.

"I'm okay," Jack said.

"Please stop telling me you're okay," Lora said, tears forming in her eyes.

"I have to go, she doesn't leave me," Jack said, taking her hands into his.

"What going on Jack, please…" a sob escaped her lips. "I don't know what to do. I don't know what to believe anymore," Lora said.

"I've always been in your heart," Jack said. "Can you sing for me, one more time?" Lora stared into his eyes, tears rolling down her cheeks as his grip got tighter.

"I can touch you babe, are you really here?" Lora said in a low tone.

"She's coming," Jack said, the amount of water dripping increased till it looked like he was under a waterfall.

"Who?" Lora asked.

"I have to go." He said in a deep voice, and then his body fell like water, leaving Lora's hand in the air.

"Lora." Jenny came out of the kitchen. "Oh my God, what the hell?" Jenny asked, looking at the pool of water.

"He's gone," Lora said, staring blankly at the wet ground.

Rock Dream Scene 6 big rock fest. Lora transforms in front of thousands, fire, panic.

A mass of punks and rockers gathered everwhere. Some took actions like mud battles, at some spots fire explosions surprised the crowd. Behind the stage hard rock stars relaxed in groups.

A loud sound came from the stage boxes, it was a greeting from off just an kick off for the big rock party. One rocker bike was riding in front oft he stage leaving fire behind. The star band appeared on the stage. The crowd started screaming.

Jenny and Lora looked at each other in the backstage, while enjoying the moment.

„That's how it feels to be a star. Amazing. This more than love." Lora sait to Jenny, looking back at the stage.

"Yep, its worship." Jenny answered.

„I hate you." Lora turned to Jenny again.

„I know." Jenny replied, with a smile.

A stage consultant approached to them, "No words, no statements, just perform, everybody hates you, but they love your song, so just show up after, after next band, so if you see water and fire, jump out of hell."

"Thank you, Jimmy. Please carry up energy blocks," Jenny responded to him.

"The next band arriving on the stage are Scorpsserum," Jimmy informed.

Lora filledagain, the same feeling in her belly. She leaved them, moving behind the stage to get some air. She watche as her skin began to chnage. Jenny looked over to Lora while keeping her conversation with Jim. Lora collapsed to the ground, starting to throw up, just like the action before transformation. Jenny leved Jimmy behind, "Wait, Jimmy."

Somebody grabed Jimmy to follow, Jimmy looked back tot he girls, realizing the troubles with Lora.

„Baby, oh no, its looks ugly," Jenny spoke to Lora taking Loras hand. Jenny leaned down and hugged Lora. At that moment she knew and was ready to give up her dream, starting to cry, so Lora can't see.

„I fully messed up, sorry babe, I'm a goner." Lora filled as Jenny's tear fallen on her skin.

„It's my foul, we should break." Jenny replied.

„No yet, babe, we are RELY, we made a lot of horror together, Lora started to cry too, both girls got a lot of black smearing in the faces. Lora looked over to Jenny, starting to get more angry, her skin more transformed.

Lora tried to get up "Let's make the last…," Jimmy interupted her "Are you ok? So now girls it's your turn". They both got up, Jimmy saw the first signs of Loras transformation and asked, "But if you are not ready?!...

Both made their way tot he stage, leaving Jimmy behind. They both saw the way to the stage, people formed a tunnel on the backstage in therms of nonnor, outhere the mass called, "Rely, Rely, lyly, Rely, Relyy…"

They held their breath again and slowly moved on tot he middle oft h stage.

Jenny wanted they cross slowly the fingers to hold hands together, just as her really sister, she asked Lora, "How it feels? Hard to believe – if the dream is going to be real."

This moment a big fire rised up in front of the stage upon on the water. The show can start, but the signs for Lora big fail just started, her skin curse growing, eyes glowing.

They appeared on stage the mass started screaming. This moment a thunder sound hited the universe.

Rely started to perform. Lora started to sing, searching for Jake in the crowd. She saw him, he stood between the fans, without a move just looking at her.

The crowd loved the song. If the refrain began, people have begun to perish in Trans. Lora slowly lost control of her body and went slowly to her knees. Jenny glanced over at her and the same moment several giant lightings struck the stage and the crowd. In the background the wind was coming near to the area with a very violent power. A tornado was growing on the place, wind and fire like a fast demon dancing around, closing the circle around rock junkies.

A panic had broken out in the crowd. Some lighting balls full of electricity moved slowly just hitting wet girls and guys. Once Light balls got to energy sources and started to grow.

Lora stoped to sings, she transformed fully. After the panic had broken out in the crowd, only a few people noticed that there was something wrong with Lora on stage. Some people caught a fire while they were running.

Folks from backstage looked at the horror happening with Lora escaped from stage. One big lightning hitted the technical side of the big stage again, causing a huge fire.

Jenny wanted to stay with Lora, but security evacuated her because of fire. A security guard turned around, wanting to help Lora. When he saw Lora, he was scared and jumped off the stage.

It was everywhere a hell on earth. The storm got stronger with a lot of flashes and powerfull wind, making Festival territory to a deadly place for every one. Trough the panic a lot of people were pressed to the edge, falling down into river.

Lora fully transformed into the beast, started to hunt the people, who tryed to save hinself in water. It was wrong and deadly decision. The people died everywhere. The heavy rock fest turned to a very heavy satanic dinner.

Last descent.

Although, while she kills, she has no control over it. The guilt that comes afterward, the memory of their screams, the way they writhed beneath her devilishly tight grip is too much for her to bear. The only way to stop the curse is to die, she is the Loreley now.

The only way to stop Loreley was to put her own life at an end.

Lora bit her lip, staring down at the bloodstain on her shoes. Chest heaving shakily, she furrowed her brows and straightened her back. She wouldn't give in so easily, she wouldn't let Loreley win, she wouldn't let her hurt anyone else.

With nothing but the clothes on her back, the young woman marched back to the hospital she had been to far too many times.

Upon arrival, Lora demanded to speak with a doctor, although the woman at reception was frazzled by her adamants, she was in no position to refuse. The nurse leads her towards a room, a room filled with enough medical staff for Lora to feel more secure.

"My name is Lora. I am the cause for all the deaths by the pier, I'm a siren" she breathed out shakily, brushing off the shocked looks she received in return at her odd admission.

"I want to kill- I want to eat" she choked out, gums aching with the need to feast.

"I want to eat all of you"

Startled into action, the medical staff stormed towards the young girl, strong hands gripping onto her biceps like a vice, preventing her from attacking just as she was about to transform. They dragged Lora's body over to the nearby stretcher, forcing her body down and strapping her in place firmly.

The young woman cried out, snapping her jaws at those who dared to come close, desperate for an eager bite of their flesh.

The head doctor grabbed a sedative from the nearby table, hurriedly uncapping it and jabbing the young woman in the side of the neck. She cried out in pain, hissing and snapping her jaws at him, though within moments, her movements had become sloppy.

Through her blurry eyes, she stared up at the man who had jabbed her. It had been the doctor she had killed on the final day of her transformation. Why was he here?

As her hazy eyes glanced around the room, she saw them, the patients in straight jackets leaning back against the walls, there was the young man she had just killed. The nurse off to the side looked remarkably like her dear friend Jenny. Next to the nurse stood Ursula.

As Lora stared at the patients and medical staff around her, they all looked so familiar, they were all the people that she had feasted upon.

"We've been through this, Lora" the doctor spoke up, his voice sounded distant as the morphine slowly began to kick in.

"Loreley isn't real, sirens aren't real, none of it is real, just get some rest alright? Rest."

The more he spoke, the further she drifted away. Her eyes closed briefly, too heavy to keep open, the face of the blurry medical staff staring down at her.

When Lora looked slowly to the side, she was alone again, tied to the bed, the bed was surrounded by water. She was surrounded by endless water. The bed slowly dipped into the water. Tied down and powerless, Lora watched as she plunged into the depths.

Encased in the cold, murky water. The sight before her an all too familiar one, in the distance, the rotting wooden planks of an old ship. Around her, never-ending water in every direction.

The only difference this time?

As she drifted further into the deep.

She was no longer afraid when she slowly descended into the depths. She was home again. Hope filled her heart. Someone touched her hand, she looked down and saw Jack free her hands and free Lora from the bed.

His loving eyes met her eyes. She looked beautiful. They took their hands and floated weightlessly. Lora hugged him. They are together again. She has found him, and she will never let him go again. He is her only love and they stay here together deep under the water forever.

EVE SCHAUBERG

LORELEY

Rock Siren
2020

Loreley is more than just a myth, Lora sets out again to find out the truth about who Loreley really is. She continues to fight for her dream and her dead love. Learn more in the upcoming chapter 2 of the Loreley saga. Win the upcoming book from the Loreley Saga Chapter 2, just tell us why you would like to read Chapter 2: love@loreleybook.com

www.loreleybook.com

Zeitfracht Medien GmbH
Ferdinand-Jühlke-Straße 7
99095 Erfurt, Deutschland
produktsicherheit@kolibri360.de